Botafogo

GITANO
26 MAY 2006
VANCOUVER

To my Dear Granny Betsy, who passed away on January 27th 2007. I dedicate this story to you.

Corcovado

Um cantinho e um violão
Este amor, uma canção
Pra fazer feliz a quem se ama

Muita calma pra pensar
E ter tempo pra sonhar

Da janela vê-se o Corcovado
O Redentor que lindo

Quero a vida sempre assim com você perto de mim
Até o apagar da velha chama

E eu que era triste
Descrente deste mundo
Ao encontrar você eu conheci
O que é felicidade meu amor

O que é felicidade, o que é felicidade

Composição: Antonio Carlos Jobim

Chapter I

The Beautiful and the Ugly

"Why are some born into excess and opportunity, while others are left to live in poverty and despair, without any hope for better?"

"Is it through accident, or through divine intervention that only some have access to education, liberty, and justice, while the rest struggle to keep a roof over their heads?

There is no answer; however, as surely as the sun rises and falls, and the seasons pass from one to the next, there will always be richer and there will always be poorer.

Brazil is testimony to this mystery of human existence. It was there that I began this story, in Rio de Janeiro, Brazil's cultural and social centre, where worlds collide in an incredible cacophony of cast and class. Rio de Janeiro: a crowded global city of nearly fifteen million people jammed together between mountain and sea, in one of the densest concentrations of human matter on earth.

To the untrained eye this city is paradise on earth, uplifting even the most sorrowful of souls with her soaring mountains coated with layers of lush tropical vegetation, rising above a brilliant turquoise sea. Yet at a more profound level, when the clouds shroud the city in mist, she transforms into a dark and sweaty land of melancholy as oppressive heat, persistent drizzle, and heavy pollution coat the city in a convoluted layer of misery. Under the clouds, Rio de Janeiro drifts into a state of solitude, her inhabitants holing themselves up inside their abodes, shivering from the lack of light as they wait impatiently for the sun's return - *Cariocas* are creatures of the sun, worshiping her vitality in hedonistic millions as they flock to the beaches, escaping from the realities of their daily lives.

Rio de Janeiro is a microcosm of the world, a violent tapestry of rich and poor. Twenty four hours a day, seven days a week, three hundred sixty five days a year they cross each others paths - rich and poor, old and young, peaceful and violent, loving and deceitful, black and white, good and evil - the world in one place.

This is a story about human beings, their reality, their daily struggle to improve the lot that they were unwillingly served the day they were born, striving to survive at all cost while in search of happiness, one day longer, one day at a time in Rio de Janeiro.

Divinity

The weather was hot, real hot, as hot as Rio de Janeiro should get at the end of December, as the city melts its way towards yet another season of Carnivals and celebrations, which come with the start of another new year. With Christmas gone, minds turn towards the looming arrival of three days of intense hedonistic celebrations that precede Catholicism's rituals of Lent – forty days to the death of Christ.

The streets were filled with shoppers flowing in and out of shopping malls and onto crowded streets, some hauling packages from the generic big-box department stores, others, obviously richer, carrying bags sporting the names of some of Brazil's most famous designer labels: *Osklen*, *Redley*, to name but a few. Street vendors, or *camelos*, blocked the sidewalks with trinkets and cheap gadgets to pawn off to enterprising shoppers, while flocks of bare-footed street children from the hilltop slums worked the crowds, innocently slipping the odd garment or wallet from any unsuspecting shopper caught daydreaming. Cars swarmed the streets, zigzagging between the ever present grid-lock of buses blocking the main thoroughfares of nearly every part of the city - the sounds of engines and car horns filling the air, occasionally punctuated with the cacophony of sirens as either a police car or an ambulance lurched difficultly through openings in the traffic.

A typical Rio de Janeiro summer's day - madness under a scorching sun.

Walking amidst the chaos was a clean-shaven, slender, middle-aged man, dressed in a short-sleeve white-collar shirt with a simple black tie, a pair of heavy grey trousers, polished black shoes, and a shiny black briefcase in one hand, with an umbrella in the other. He stepped a steady gate, gazing ahead through the throngs of shoppers and businessmen crowding the streets and crossing before him.

Patiently weaving through the crowds, he walked to the bus stop, taking his place calmly in the short queue for the next bus from *Copacabana* to *Ipanéma*. Despite the oppressive heat he had an air of determination, in marked contrast to the glazed looks of exhausted commuters standing in silence beside him. His face, like everyone else's, was covered in a fine sheen of sweat, which he wiped away using a fresh white handkerchief hanging from the pocket of his freshly ironed dress pants.

A lonely old woman standing beside him mumbled how hot it was, apparently wanting to strike up some sort of conversation. He ignored her, preferring to stare glassily ahead at the unwavering passing traffic, inching forward in noisy ebbs and flows with the changing of the traffic lights.

After a short wait, the next bus to *Ipanéma* pulled up at the stop, pausing to let all the passengers aboard before pulling out into the sea of cars and buses, joining thousands of others in an unbearable crawl towards *Ipanéma*.

An hour later he stood in silence outside a plain white church on *Ipanema's* main thoroughfare. The building was non-descript – other than the dried-up Christmas decorations at the front door, there was nothing to indicate any affiliation with God. Bowing his head gently, he stepped discreetly inside.

The interior of the church was warm and dark, with the subtle odour of unwashed bodies. He stood by the front door, pausing briefly to adjust to the light as he glanced at the faces filling the rows of plain wooden pews. He found a seat in an empty pew at the back of the church, putting his black briefcase and umbrella on the floor beside him, as he quietly joined in the midday mass already underway.

The church minister, an immense black man with thick horn-rimmed spectacles, was singing vigorously from the front of the room, his face covered in sweat, as his pastoral robe clung to his gigantic heaving body. He had the room hypnotized, his bellowing voice chanting hymns as his loyal followers sang blindly along.

After several minutes the sermon ebbed, giving way to more open standing prayer. Unnoticed by the crowds of worshippers, the man opened his black briefcase and pulled out a shiny object, slipping it gently into his front pocket. Closing the briefcase, he stepped out from seat at the back of the hall to walk crisply up to the front pews. There he looked at a tall redheaded young man standing in the front row, whose face was intently focused on the minister at the front of the room, disconnected from his surroundings.

The man paused, his white short-sleeve collar shirt soaked in sweat, his face devoid of any expression; then, without a moment's hesitation, he lifted the revolver and fired five bullets at point blank range into the young man's face, before turning the gun on himself, firing the remaining shot into his skull in front of the entire room.

Silence.

The ensuing moments melted in the air, as pieces of human flesh and blood splattered about, covering walls, pews, floors, and bystanders in the congregation.

Then, like the breaking of a glass, the silence shattered, and the first high-pitched screams of terror and pandemonium erupted from the pews. Stunned, the minister stalled in mid-sentence, dropping to the floor in fear, while several ladies in the adjacent seats fainted, and others, screaming, attempted to force themselves out of the seething mass of struggling survivors.

Several men near the victim tried to pull him from the floor, rushing to initiate CPR, only to discover that his face was no more. Others around him struggled with cell phones, possibly trying to contact an ambulance. Within minutes the church was empty, the men who had tried to save the victim fleeing with rest once they realized he was no more.

Within the hour a media circus had surrounded the church, as police, forensic agents, paramedics, and curious onlookers rushed about. On the street the traffic dropped from a crawl to a complete standstill, as not a single car, bus, or motorcycle was able to move, creating a line of traffic and noisy frustration stretching back block after block in the unfettered mid-summer heat.

Chapter II

Luis - Paris one year earlier

"Varig Flight 932 to Rio de Janeiro is now calling passengers seated in business executive and first class to board. *Varig vol 932 destination Rio de Janeiro appelle tout passager en classe d'affaires ou en première classe à bord….*"

Luis looked up, gathered his briefcase and boarding card in one hand, and his copy of Le Monde in the other, and walked hurriedly to the boarding counter.

"Yes, Mr. De Silva welcome onboard. May I take your coat and belongings?"

Exhausted, Luis collapsed back into his seat, loosened his tie, and drifted off into a daze. These business trips were tiring affairs he wished he no longer had to perform - there was no pleasure in flying fifteen hours to be imprisoned in plastic and undistinguishable hotel boardrooms, listening to nameless lawyers and accountants in various cities of the world.

He preferred to be at home in his apartment on the seaside, the only sounds those of the singing of the birds from his rooftop garden, and the noise of the surf rolling in off the Atlantic. He longed for those magnificent morning walks down along the seaside in *Ipanéma*, precious moments of solitude when he was able to forget the worries of the world.

"Sir, for dinner service, do you have a preference for red or white wine?"

Snapped back to reality, Luis looked up at the pleasant looking stewardess and her two bottles of wine. "I'll have the white please, thank you."

Alone again, he drifted back to his thoughts, forgetting the chores of work, as he sipped on the light glass of chilled white wine. His mind was laden with thoughts, too many in fact, so much so that even the irresistible calling of sleep was at times not enough for his mind to shut down for even just a few hours. There were concerns, his family, the direction of his business interests, his own health.

He thought of his ex-wife, Margaret, and the marriage they thankfully no longer shared, replaced by a divorce that they, or more so he, had had to manage. There was no other way to describe Margaret than as completely unreasonable. The divorce had been difficult, sending his health downhill, but what was worse was that she did not seem to take no for an answer, calling him over and over again to nag, threat, and complain. Up until just a few weeks ago she was phoning him as much as a dozen times a day, obliging him to change his cell phone number several times, and his secretaries to invent all sorts of stories, so he could find some peace.

How on earth had he ever ended up marrying such a woman? All she wanted was money, and more and more of it every day.

Fortunately money was of no significance to Luis, he had so much of it that his accountants had no idea how to really calculate his true net worth, which was probably a good thing, since it meant the Brazilian taxman had an even harder job determining just how much Mr. De Silva should be paying on a yearly basis. Luis had everything, expensive clothes, fast cars, and several luxurious properties in global cities around the world, including Sao Pãolo, Buenos Aires, Paris, and New York. He also had holiday houses in North East Brazil, Monte Carlo, and the Alps, and he was now onto his fourth yacht, a magnificent 125-meter fully staffed luxury ship with everything set to perfection.

Of course there were also the children from that absurd marriage of his - two boys to be exact. One, by the name of David, was at the *Universidade Federal do Rio de Janeiro*, completing a doctorate in journalism and economics, whilst entertaining various teaching and research offers from top institutes, including the World Bank in New York and the World Health Organization in Lyon.

David was the almost perfect son, who two years ago had told his parents he was gay and that his supposed housemate of some five years was in fact his lover and confidant. Realizing the importance of keeping his son in his life, Luis had accepted his boy's decision, and over the years came to respect David's partner João, who was every bit as intelligent and amusing as his son.

Yet unlike Luis, Margaret did not accept David's decision, immediately sending her son for all sorts of medical and psychiatric tests, only to erupt in frustration when the doctors said there was nothing they could do to fix the disease. In fury she had turned on her son, telling him he was no longer welcome in their house. With the whole fiasco completely out of hand, Luis, already at knives with his wife, told her that if she imposed such conditions on their son he would divorce her.

That was the beginning of the end of their horrid twenty-three year marriage, and as far as Luis was concerned it was for the best. With their marriage finished, Luis turned his full attention to his son. He supported the boy and his partner João, encouraging them in their studies, and using his influence in legal circles to isolate his wife from the couple.

The failure of their marriage had been difficult for their other son, who by nature was more of a challenge than David. Eduardo had been difficult ever since the first days of school, often coming home with warnings from teachers, and constantly bringing one new governess after another to tears.

As the years passed, Eduardo began to run up a list of scholastic shortcomings, failing every program that Luis had paid for, including a brief foray at a local private university. The young man's interests strayed far from the classroom, leaning instead towards martial arts and frequent parties with inauspicious friends in *Leblon*, Barra, and *Ipaněma.* There was no communication between Luis and his younger son, except when Eduardo needed more money to finance his obvious addictions to women, drugs, parties, and dubious business interests. All that Luis could do was use his political influence to ensure his youngest son remained clear of the law.

Luis had no idea why David was such a success, and Eduardo such a failure. Was it due to the years of neglect Eduardo had suffered while his father was on business overseas and his mother at her fashion parties with the ladies at the Jockey Club, or was it Luis' lack of acceptance of Eduardo's disinterest in books and education and his preference for martial arts, or simply put, was it his obvious preference for David?

What was known was that Eduardo had not taken his parents' divorce well, probably because he was forced to spend most of the time shuttling between his parents' and grandparents' apartments until things were sorted out. He blamed his brother for the collapse of his parents' marriage and showed no shame in his disgust for his brother's lifestyle. The animosity between the two was so deep that they never talked, and the year and a half that separated them was like a cultural and intellectual divide.

Luis' thoughts drifted back and forth in an endless analytical spiral, from his sons to his estranged wife and then once again back to his sons – finding no answers. Eventually the combination of sheer exhaustion and four glasses of wine and a warm meal sent him drifting into yet another short and restless night's sleep.

He awoke to the sound of the captain's voice over the PA as the announcement was made first in French, and then in Portuguese that the aircraft was on its approach to Rio de Janeiro. He opened his shutter blind and looked out across the blue sky, scanning the land below as he tried to make out his beloved "*Cidade Marvilhosa*". As they approached the city, the cluttered combination of mountains, hilltops, *favela*s, and apartments began to emerge - Rio de Janeiro, chaos in paradise.

The sounds of the engine grew heavier, and the cabin lights dimmed as the flight attendants took their seats in preparation for the imminent landing. The plane hurtled forward, as cluttered slums and squatter housing swarmed below under the rumble of jet engines, eventually giving way to open runway, just in time as the wheels met tarmac, ending yet another of Luis' tiring forays outside of his beloved Brazil. "Brasil how I missed you, *saudades de você*". He thought to himself.

Exhausted, and happy to be home, Luis slipped into the back of his Mercedes, leaving his driver Carlos to deal with the complexities of Rio de Janeiro's traffic. The weather was marvellously hot, so much of a contrast to the two weeks of dreary winter skies in Paris and New York.

He pulled his phone from his coat, anxious to speak to his favourite son.

"David, its papa! I'm back from Europe and America! How are you my boy?"

"Ah papa, welcome home! You must be tired no?"

"A bit of course, though I did sleep a little on the plane. Never mind me though; did you get any news about your applications?" said Luis.

" Thrilling news…my defence date has been moved forward, the department wants to support my offer from the World Bank in New York!"

"Congratulations my boy, and João what are his plans?"

"He's decided he will come with me to the United States. The university came through yesterday and has offered him a teaching position as an adjunct professor!"

"Hmm sounds like an excellent reason to celebrate. Why don't the two of you come over for dinner tonight? I will see what Maria can put together."

"Sure papa, I'll give João a call, but I don't see it being a problem! Just don't forget, no meat!"

"Okay my boy," he laughed. "I'll see you both tonight! Love you!"

"Love you papa!"

Luis shut the phone and lay back, his tie plastered to the seat over his shoulder, and his collar loosened, giving him a definitively dishevelled air.

"Carlos, phone Maria and tell her to prepare a vegetarian dinner for three tonight on the terrace. As soon as I get home I think I'll be going off for a nice walk along the seaside, and a swim, damn it I need a swim..."

Carlos slipped out of view - the screen separating driver and passenger raised - leaving Luis in silence, with only the subtle noise of passing traffic and the hum of the Mercedes engine. His mind wondered off, staring absently at the suburban sprawl as it drifted silently by: one muddy street after another, a sea of disjointed red brick and mortar with thousands of satellite dishes and endless clothing lines.

Amongst the houses he caught glimpses of children playing football on the streets with whatever they could find – soda cans, tennis balls, and if they were lucky, a stitched together football. They were flickering images of joy amongst what was so certainly misery and hopelessness.

My God Brazil is complex. How could one ever explain such a sight to an executive in some distant boardroom in New York or Paris. Half of those fools only saw numbers on balance sheets, and with those numbers they seemed to have the confidence to make decisions that broke and made the lives of millions around the world. We are all connected, from the poorest of the poor on these streets, to the richest of the rich at perfect public schools in Chelsea.

He thought of his own youth as an only child in the late fifties and sixties, and how as early as the age of ten his father had taken him by trolley to the city centre, giving him glimpses into the other side of Brazil, a distant reality from the swimming pools and private schools of the south side of the city. His father, despite being born into privilege, took a deep interest in the state of his country. While he was alive, the man had constantly bemoaned how years of government mismanagement and protectionist regimes had done nothing other than funnel public funds into foreign bank accounts.

Luis remembered his father's angry frustration when they drove into the suburbs, how the man complained bitterly of how vast the problem was and yet how little people really seemed to care. "I am alone in this, none of my so-called friends even want to hear what I have to say," he lamented.

The incognito visits to the suburbs and growing *favela*s were an important part of Luis' education, as his impassioned father sought to expose his son to his true obsession: the work outside of boardrooms and political shoulder rubbing. As his father liked to say, 'The rich have a civic duty to care for the poor. That is why rather than giving my damn tax money to the fat cows in Brasilia, I prefer spending it here in Rio de Janeiro, building schools and houses for people like these. It is our responsibility to care for them, because otherwise they have no one…"

Indeed that is what his father did – construct houses and infrastructure for thousands of marginalized suburban working people, people who had barely a cent and probably no possibility of bettering themselves. His father's work brought opportunities to the hopeless, and as the local police would testify, crime and violence was dramatically lower in neighbourhoods where his father's projects had been initiated.

It was those first striking images that instilled in Luis the same desire to contribute as his father had done. As he grew older, in the late seventies as a student of journalism at PUC in Rio de Janeiro, he initiated his own projects involving the financial support of his friends' parents. The idea behind his work was to promote awareness and activism amongst the elite as to the burgeoning problem of Rio de Janeiro's ballooning migrant social underclass. In some ways his projects worked; however, he realized that they were simply too small to have much impact without the political openness of a vibrant democracy.

For this reason he chose to go abroad, where he believed that free of the complexities of Brazil, he would be able to explore solutions, while at the same time learn more about the world outside of his country.

Studying for a Ph. D. in economics in New York, Luis garnered the support of various local organizations to encourage foreign students and academics to visit Brazil and contribute to the betterment of Brazilians, while at the same time raising awareness of the issues of corruption, dictatorship, and poverty in the international community.

As Luis saw it, the poor required so little to make a dramatic improvement in their lives - even small contributions bringing foreign students into contact with youth could be enough to save yet another youngster from drifting into the growing underworld of the drug cartels that ran both the suburbs and the hilltop slums, or *favela*s. For foreign students a visit to Brazil opened eyes to the realities of the world, perhaps enough to enlighten them before they embarked on careers in banking and finance in "The City" or on Wall Street.

In 1980, at the age of twenty-five, Luis returned home with his Ph. D. incomplete and the unexpected responsibility of taking charge of his father's enterprises. The man he had looked up to for so many years had passed away suddenly, broken by the frustration of fighting corrupt military and marginally democratic governments. Governments that showed little interest in solving the country's social and economic problems that were making business increasingly difficult to do.

Luis would never complete his graduate studies, as the weight of responsibility soon pinned him down to focusing his energy on building the family's fortunes. Added to that, one off his father's dreams became reality, as in the mid 80's the country made a significant shift back to democracy, convincing Luis he could achieve more as an influential businessman actively involved in the democratization process, as opposed to an academic isolated in America.

Many years had gone by since his father's death. Brazil had successfully passed from years of dictatorship and military rule to a gradual installation of multiparty rule; however, much to his frustration, rather than reduce corruption and bring opportunities to the poor, the intervening years only worsened the gap between rich and poor.

This gap was what was visible from his car window, as they rolled along the cluttered airport highway in through the city towards the more affluent and comfortable neighbourhoods in the *Zona Sul*; the neighbourhoods that New York bankers and Hollywood film stars believed Rio de Janeiro was, and not the filthy sprawling suburban cesspools that were the reality.

Carlos

Carlos glanced over his shoulder at his boss, before the black screen separating driver from passenger was raised. Luis looked exhausted, his suit wrinkled from too much travel, his blue eyes dulled and surrounded by greyness, even his silvery mop of hair had lost its shine, falling unkempt across his brow.

"The rigours of international business were not for the faint hearted,' thought Carlos. Yet despite the hardship, why was it that Mister de Silva never seemed to be at peace. So strange, after all the man had so much of everything to satisfy every material desire.

Perhaps the man's decline was because he never stopped working, driven by what no longer seemed to be a passion, but rather a duty, as the complexities of his business arrangements made it more or less impossible for him to find any time or place to just escape.

Carlos was deeply respectful of Mr. De Silva: not only was he his boss, he was also his mentor and trusted friend, a man of great generosity who had shown him a sure path in life. Mr. De Silva's kindness had opened the doors to more reputable schools for Carlos' daughters and had helped organize the purchase of the family's home in *Tijuca*, which allowed them to escape the crowded conditions of their old rental apartment in *Copacabana.* The man's kindness had allowed Carlos to earn a decent living, affording his children opportunities they would never have had if their father had of gone the same way as his old friends.

Carlos was born to lower class parents who had called home amongst the sprawling suburban neighbourhoods in Rio de Janeiro's Northern and Eastern suburbs. It was a place of poverty, crime, and violence, where the city's forgotten poor struggled to survive. Where he had grown up was perhaps completely unimaginable for people like Mr. De Silva, and besides his work as an activist, all his boss probably knew about life in the suburbs was what he saw from the window of a passing car or aeroplane.

His childhood home had been a shanty affair, his room made from bare brick and wooden construction, which he shared with four of his older brothers. Of his family, two of his brothers were long since passed away, having been brutally murdered by drug barons that ruled the streets by day and night. His oldest brother Marcos, a retired policeman, had been paralysed from the waste down after a gunfight with kidnappers left him and his colleague bloodied but still alive. Marcos had returned home, after his wife had run off with his two daughters and another man, never to be seen again.

His brother's return to the family household had been a solemn affair that the family accepted without question. Everyone in the household considered Marcos a hero, who deserved their support as he struggled to come to terms with his physical handicap. Carlos, being the youngest of the brothers took to caring for his eldest sibling, wheeling him from place to place, getting his hair cut, ensuring he remained healthy. Their relationship grew strong over the years, as his brother ceaselessly told him to stay in school and to work hard to escape the poverty of the suburbs. His brother was a positive influence, acting as a counter balance to the overwhelming hopelessness of life amongst Rio's poor.

Under Marcos' wing, Carlos excelled at school, showing his natural ability for academics and love for mathematics and chemistry. His brother encouraged him, telling him to avoid those who had taken the wrong path in life. "Through goodness and honesty one can succeed" was his brother's constant reminder to Carlos.

Carlos was the last of eight children, and as a result had always received the leftovers of whatever his older siblings had worn or used over the years. His parents worked hard at what they did. His mother, known by her friends as Maria, was a small and simple illiterate black woman from Brazil's north. She never laughed or smiled, spending most of her time unnoticed in silence. Only in the few short weeks before Carnival, when Rio de Janeiro seemed to drown in the sounds of *Samba*, did she seem to be happy.

Maria travelled hours every day to clean houses in the posh neighbourhoods located in the southern part of the city. In the early hours of the morning, long before the sun had even risen, she arose from bed, beginning her long solitary journey into the city on nothing more than coffee and white bread. For safety she met a colleague on the street who also worked in town, and the two of them negotiated the muddy streets together in silence to the nearest bus.

At times, when his mother's friend was too sick to work, she awoke one of her sons to join her for the day so not to wander the streets alone. Since Carlos was the youngest, it was often he who was chosen to join his mother. He relished those journeys into the city, as they allowed him to witness things unimaginable in the despair of the suburbs - teeming streets filled with fancy cars, businessmen dressed in suits and fancy hats, fashionably clad women walking groomed dogs, street vendors punctuating the air with their cries; all under the shadows of towering office buildings and luxury apartments.

His mother worked in a plush apartment, home to some wealthy businessman who never seemed to be there. Instead it was Silvia the live-in maid who met them at the front door, riding with them up the service elevator to the top floor and the marvellous views across *Botafogo* Bay to Pão de Açucar - views that only wealth afforded.

Silvia, despite being strict in her routine, generally left Carlos' mother alone to work, giving out simple verbal instructions at the beginning of the day as to what needed to be done, and interrupting only for lunch, or if one of the sofas or carpets needed to be moved. As for Carlos, he enjoyed sitting alone in the lounge, gazing out the window at the beach, his imagination inventing games as he idly passed the day away.

The daydreaming ended at five as they took the service elevator back down to street level, joining the crowds of commuters rushing back through the city to the north, where the working-class suburbs lay.

While the journey was an adventure for Carlos, he knew his mother did it every day, six days a week, fifty-two weeks of the year, the only pause being for Carnival, Christmas and New Year. He never ceased to admire his mother's determination, and her suffering fuelled his desire to better himself and his family, so that maybe someday she too would be able to live in so beautiful a flat by the seaside.

His father's work was no better than his mother's. He worked day shifts for the city, cleaning Rio's downtown streets - picking up rubbish from over-filled litter cans. Flavio, as he was known, earned a pittance, barely a few cents more than his wife. The man spoke little of his work, preferring to drown his sorrows in wafts of thick tobacco smoke, which spiralled from his hand-rolled cigarettes. Rarely did any of the brothers speak to their father, preferring to address their worries to Maria, who if she thought it to be of enough importance, would raise the matter with her husband. Flavio's distance from the rest of the family was surely a reflection of his despair with a life of misery and impotence, a life he had been unwillingly served through the accident of birth.

With the passage of the years Carlos' parents had both long since passed away, leaving the five remaining brothers largely separated, rarely meeting for family events. In fact for the past four New Year's they had not performed their traditional family gathering, letting time and responsibilities allow them to drift apart. Yet this did not sadden Carlos, rather his devotion shifted entirely towards new responsibilities for his own family, his job, and his service to God.

He believed deeply in God, that it was the Almighty that had shone on him, giving him good fortune and finally breaking the cycle of poverty and violence that had been so a part of his family through the generations. He also believed it had been the will of God that had brought Mr. de Silva into his life, and he felt deeply indebted for the Lord's kindness. In return he and his family attended church regularly, adopting the New Evangelical Church as their place of prayer and worship. They played a significant role in the congregation: his wife baking for community events, Carlos volunteering with the church committee, and his daughters partaking in youth activities.

Yet Carlos' attention to God did not stem directly from his childhood poverty and the tragic life of the family he had been born into, rather it was during a particularly bleak and dark period of his life that he connected with his spirituality.

He was fifteen at the time, and had returned home from another day of school, dodging the raindrops as he rushed home to tell his brother Marcos how he had scored the highest marks in his class for his Portuguese exam. The house was strangely quiet, unusual since Marcos often left the radio on in the kitchen, as he tended to his small collection of flowers in the family's tiny backyard.

Carlos remembered calling out, "*Marcos, Marcos onde esta* – where are you?"

He found his brother lifeless in his bedroom, his wrists slit as he lay in a bath of bloody soiled sheets and flies. Beside his body was a suicide note: testimony to his brother's solitude and loss of independence - a tragic silenced cry of frustration and hopelessness. Carlos destroyed the note, choosing never to share it with his parents or his other living brothers. In the darkness of the room he sat crying in the stillness beside his brother, waiting for his family to come home.

In the weeks following Marcos' suicide Carlos began missing more and more school days, finally electing to drop out, deciding that education was a pointless exercise, which would never free him from his miserable existence. He began to spend most of his days revelling in parties in the emerging shantytowns above the wealthy neighbourhoods of *Leme* and *Copacabana*, far away from home in the suburbs, while also doing petty drug runs for local drug lords. With each passing day his tie to his parents faded, and the words of his late brother Marcos, "Through goodness and honesty one can succeed", seemed to fade away to nothing.

Six months after his brother's death, he decided to abandon his family's overcrowded home for the freedom of the streets, sharing a house with his new friends in *Laranjeiras*, a hilltop neighbourhood close to the city centre.

Away from school and the watch of his family, he drifted into dubious social circles, descending into the depths of Rio's criminal underworld, whilst flirting from time to time with the federal police. Carlos' friends were from poor and uneducated backgrounds, often raised on the streets of the city's burgeoning suburbs and hilltop *favelas*, where jobs were few, and the best way to make a living was by peddling drugs to rich kids in *Copacabana* and *Botafogo*, or ripping off foreign tourists on the beach.

He and his new friends were driven by one objective: find the easiest way to escape poverty. They felt no remorse in what they did, believing a society that had shown them no justice, deserved no justice in return. Drugs sold well, and Carlos and his friends began to enjoy an improved standard of living, riding taxis about the city, shopping for new clothes in the same rich neighbourhoods where his mother cleaned apartments, and experimenting in the delights of desperate prostitutes that lined the night time streets in the city. His newfound independence and economic freedom changed him, convincing him that his ruthless ways were a justifiable means for him to attain a level of wealth impossible to have achieved otherwise.

Then one sunny August day Carlos' life changed forever.

He had been living the wild life of a school dropout for two years. His career on the other side of the law paid well, and he and his friends had moved from *Laranjeiras* over to *Santa Teresa*, a wealthier neighbourhood with fine mansions and lush gardens, affording views of the city below. *Santa Teresa* was filled with beautiful steep winding cobbled streets and plazas, lined with pretty fences and majestic palm trees that swayed in the wind. The neighbourhood was quiet, an inviting welcome from the bustle of a booming city below. Indeed the only noises were those of a barking dog, or the occasional street trolley or passing car.

It was midday, and Carlos and his friends were walking up from the city centre, laughing and revelling after having robbed and beaten a feeble old lady, stealing her jewellery and purse on a main street just outside of the theatre district.

The walk up the hill home was a tiring one, and sweat ran in rivulets down Carlos' body.

That day the air was still and humid, not even a breeze from the city below, and the sun unusually unforgiving for a winter's day. Suddenly, out of nowhere, they were ambushed by a dozen masked federal police officers carrying shotguns and rifles.

Carlos and his friends panicked, having never been caught in such a situation with the police before. In the ensuing moments the humid air was transformed with electric tension - shouting and swearing flying from both sides.

"Drop everything now!!! *Caras, escutem*!!!!"

"On your knees now, *entendam*!!!"

"*Nossa karalho, puta*, what the fuck!!!"

"Fuck!!!"

Bang. Bang. Bang.

The police had called out for them to drop their weapons, and Carlos had thought his friends would heed the advice; however, they instead panicked, pulling out revolvers and shooting aimlessly at the flicks. The officers reacted mercilessly and with swift determination; firing packets of bullets back at them. Carlos was left unscathed; however, his two friends were killed on the spot, their bodies ripped apart by the onslaught of flying metal bullets.

Carlos was the only one who did not pull a gun, because he had forgotten his at home, and the only one who was left untouched – alive. The police took him into custody and he was detained for six weeks, without questioning, in a federal prison. Never had he imagined what was waiting for him on the other side of those prison walls. From the freedom of the streets he found himself alone and vulnerable in a foreign world where an innocent common criminal like him, was nothing more than feeding fodder for brutality beyond imagination.

In the weeks of his imprisonment he learnt much about himself, discovering that the hard shell he had built through crime was nothing more than a tender coating that with the horrors of an overcrowded penitentiary simply cracked and fell away. The memories of friends no more, of his brother Marcos and his kind gentle soul, of his family who had not seen or heard of in months and who probably had no idea of his fate. In a few short weeks Carlos, the angry child, was no more, and in its place was a humble young man who sought to better his ways if chance would allow him to do so.

Mysteriously, as if God had heard his prayers, he was released from prison without even a trial. At the age of eighteen he found himself back on the streets, standing on a filthy street corner in suburban Rio de Janeiro, looking back at the weed covered walls that had once contained his spirit and his soul in such misery and pain. That was the last time that Carlos would cry, the memories of weeks of horrors washing down upon him under the waves of brilliant Carioca sunshine.

Free, declared an innocent bystander due to lack of proof, Carlos Varas found himself given a second chance, the opportunity to find the path his brother Marcos had so wanted him to follow.

In the years that followed Carlos returned to school, rediscovering the wisdom of his deceased brother Marcos. He completed his collegial studies and subsequently joined the army, where first he learnt to drive tanks and armoured vehicles as a junior rank officer, before going on to take a position as a driver for senior military staff. He was a serious young man in the army, which led to his gaining favour amongst the senior staff members. Indeed while others of his level preferred to go out at night, he chose to remain in the barracks, taking time to leaf through the pages of a bible he had purchased on the day he was released from gaol.

At night, while others drank and swooned over prostitutes, Carlos read page after page of his precious book, until he was eventually able to sight entire texts from the bible. When that was not enough, he took to writing, recording his thoughts on paper - memories of his past, hopes for the future, and thoughts and words that gradually laid the foundations of the man he was to become.

While in the military he also met his wife, Isabella, a shy coffee-coloured girl of a small lower-middle class family from a town in the highlands of Sao Pãolo.

They had met by accident, or as he preferred to believe by divine intervention, on the beach on a sunny Sunday afternoon. She had been in Rio de Janeiro on holidays with her parents, when on that fateful afternoon Carlos had spotted her from a distance. Their chance meeting took place on the *calçada* where the vendors sold flowers, *Guarana*, and photographs. He had followed her up to the juice stand, catching her attention with a gentle smile, which she shyly returned.

Initially her parents had been somewhat sceptical; however, when they heard of his stable post in the military, his stellar record, and his position as a rising ranking officer, their uncertainty faded, replaced with a confidence that allowed their courting to continue.

From their first meeting began a two-year love affair between the two, at the end of which Carlos received Isabella's parents' approval for their marriage and her move to live with him in Rio de Janeiro.

His young wife was supportive of his military career, in her quiet manner attending all the functions required of a loyal army spouse. Yet Carlos knew that the earnings of a junior sergeant were vastly insufficient for him and his wife to even hope of raising a family in a better neighbourhood. Carlos deeply wanted better, working hard to impress his superiors in the hope of achieving a promotion to a higher rank and a salary, which would allow him to give more to his wife.

He was getting no younger though, and his work seemed to go unnoticed as he remained in check in his position as a professional driver, chauffeuring generals, admirals, politicians, and foreign dignitaries back and forth from various functions. The job was considerably better than anything else his colleagues had been assigned; however, it was far from exciting and it lacked the element of risk and opportunity for bravery that usually allowed for promotion. Carlos knew though, and his wife agreed, that it was too risky an affair for him to join the military's active branches, which were embarked on a shadowy role behind the political system governing the country.

Carlos and Isabella's breakthrough finally happened, when by chance one of the staff generals, who had gotten to know Carlos as a regular driver, recommended him to a wealthy Carioca industrialist who was in need of a trustful and professional driver.

That industrialist was a tall good-looking, playboy, by the name Mr. Luis De Silva.

In the years that followed Carlos worked loyally for the De Silva family, getting to know every detail of their lives. He marvelled at how different they were from his own immediate family. Watching them was like observing four elegant birds flying and darting in different directions, each shared the same nest; however, none really seemed to care for the dealings of the others.

He recalled the break-up between Mrs. De Silva and his boss. The whole affair had been most horrid, casting a pall over the family. The divorce made front page on Rio's tabloids, as the news of the feud provided a welcome respite for journalists accustomed to covering the endless drug wars in the squalors of Rio's suburbs.

Mr. De Silva finally was able to untangle himself from his marriage, buying his wife a separate house in *Gavéa* so he would no longer have to deal with her, and offering her an immense settlement, somewhat unjust given it had been she who had committed most of the mischief. Carlos had witnessed the woman's infidelity as she committed adultery with one man and then the next. It seemed as though she never tired of finding newer and younger men. Her last one, just before she and her husband finally signed the papers, was the family garden boy, a youngster of the age of eighteen.

While the De Silva's were torn apart by family ruptures, Carlos' family was the complete antithesis. He had three daughters, of whom he was immensely proud. They had a bright future, a result of Carlos' job, which gave them the benefits of excellent health care and a private school in a good neighbourhood. His eldest daughter had worked hard and had been accepted into a respectable public university to study chemistry in preparation for pharmacy. His two younger daughters excelled in music and sports and seemed destined to follow the academic path of their elder sibling.

The future seemed bright for Carlos and his family, bright indeed after so much struggle and so many years. Perhaps there really was hope for those at the bottom of society: the forgotten, the poor, the illiterate, and the disenfranchised. Perhaps, just perhaps, dreams could come true.

Isabella

Isabella trudged down the street pushing her shopping cart laden with the day's groceries. The air was still, the usual smells of pollution intermingled with the noise of street traffic, the occasional barking dog, and the familiar push and hustle of pedestrians rushing about in a never-ending frenzy. There was no hurry in her step; she realized the pointlessness of rushing one chore only to get to another, which in this case was to cook dinner.

How tired she felt, overcome by a profound sense of fatigue, her mind adrift with boredom, the result of a routine that had existed for so long that she simply could not remember anything different. The days were identical, blending into a monotonous haze, broken only by the ritual of church on Sunday morning.

Isabella's role as the family housewife, after so many years, had turned into a great deception, as she realized her religious devotion to her husband had come at an enormous cost. She was no longer a young woman, her beauty slowly fading with the passing of time. Every morning, as she rose to prepare breakfast, she would stare at her figure in the bathroom mirror, counting the lines as they spread deeper and further across her face, gradually eclipsing the last lustre of youth.

She was frustrated with her life, tired of the rigidity and perfection her husband imposed upon the household, as he lived oblivious to the emotional needs of his wife and daughters. Carlos lived in a world of fantasy, walking out the door every morning and returning for dinner - never asking a single question as to how their day had been, and never delving further than pleasantries about church or the goings on at the De Silva household.

Granted, Carlos was older than she by several years, and she had wanted to marry him as much as he her; however, in the ensuing years of marriage, the curtains of ignorance covering his eyes seemed to disconnect him from the more intimate needs of a wife, who sensed her last few years of beauty going to waste on a man blinded by devotion to ideals and work.

Carlos was not a bad man - he had provided everything his family could possibly desire. His loyal work with the De Silva family had given them relative wealth and prosperity, affording their daughters access to opportunities otherwise unattainable to people of their class. What was wrong was that her husband lacked, passion, energy, and most importantly love. After so many years of marriage, he was till an enigma to her, a man shrouded in secrecy and an unexplained past.

She knew she was, or probably already had fallen out of love with Carlos, yet somehow, out of duty, Isabella continued to play the role of a supportive and loyal wife.

Rising early in the morning to despondently stare at the bathroom mirror, followed by the trudge into the family kitchen to prepare breakfast for the household, which most of the time consisted of some sliced fruit, toast, and hard-boiled eggs. Carlos usually ate his breakfast alone and in silence, chewing absent-mindedly, while reading the morning newspaper. When he was done, his teeth freshly brushed, she took her place at the door, helping him put on his familiar black blazer and tie, stepping back as he slipped on his black leather shoes, which he kept polished and shined at the front door in strict military tradition, and waving goodbye as he slipped out the door and into the shiny black De Silva limousine.

Not a kiss, not a hug, not the slightest hint of emotion.

After Carlos had left, her three daughters grabbed the rest of the food, rushing into the kitchen on the way to the front door and another day of school. In less than a few minutes Isabella was alone: the house suddenly silent, not a single sound apart from the ticking of the kitchen clock and the hum of passing cars on the streets outside. The silence was perhaps the worst, since it was then that her mind wandered, and her thoughts began to twist and turn, tormenting her as she walked about in the grey, shadowed emptiness called home.

There was a phone in the house; however, there was really nobody to phone, especially to talk about her feelings, and in particular her sadness. All of their friends were more friends of Carlos, colleagues from the military, acquaintances from church, and other associates from work. She was nothing more than a lonely housewife, whose last sparkles of youth were rapidly fading away.

Isabella contemplated suicide, as the weeks, months, and years passed she began to imagine more vividly her own death and the attention it would bring. "Perhaps then this family will finally notice me," she thought.

She visualized herself jumping in front of a train, or hanging herself in the living room. Yet each time the moment seemed right, Isabella lost her nerve, dejectedly choosing to take the familiar shopping cart and begin the day's chores of groceries and housework.

Then one day everything changed. She was down at the waterfront minding her own business when a stranger caught her eye. A glance, a smile, a flutter, and a touch, a few words, an exchange of addresses, and then secretive midday walks along the seaside in *Botafogo*.

It had been a beautiful early December morning and her husband had gone off to work earlier than usual to pick up Mr. De Silva, as he returned from another business meeting overseas. With the arrival of nice weather, she had decided to go down to the seaside for a leisurely stroll. The idea seemed like a good one, a pleasant change in her routine, and a chance to get outside after nearly three weeks of non-stop rain.

She had taken nearly the entire morning to prepare for her walk down on the beach, putting make-up on her face, painting her lips, and picking a skirt she had secretly purchased several days earlier in the city. Dressed to her finest, she paraded herself in front of the mirror, before wandering down to the street to flag a taxi.

The seaside was alive under brilliant blue skies and fresh ocean spray, filled with vibrant energy and activity, so much of a contrast to the plainness of her middle class neighbourhood in *Tijuca*. Everywhere she looked there were people, young bikini-clad women, tall scantily dressed men, rich and poor, old and young; they were all magnificent, and they were all happy.

Joggers raced along the beach path, doing all sorts of exercises to slow the determined forces of gravity and age that ultimately showed no discrimination between rich and poor. Cyclists rushed by, not stopping for even the odd pedestrian who happened to idle too long on the bicycle path. Wherever she looked there were beautiful men and women about, and the sight of such perfection ashamed and angered her; shame because of her fading beauty, and anger for the isolated life she led with a husband she no longer loved.

Feeling self-conscious, Isabella sought something to keep her hands occupied, setting her eyes on the coconut drinks selling for one real at the nearby juice stand. Stepping up to the counter, she opened her purse, extracting a single green bill as the barman placed her drink on the counter.

Coconut water flowed through the straw, the refreshing flavour running across her palate as she joined the throngs of walkers and joggers jostling down the promenade.

Amongst the crowds, and unbeknownst to her, a young man had been watching her for some time, gazing from behind sunglasses at the unusually overdressed woman strolling along the seaside, slightly awkward and innocent for her age. Not hesitating, he appeared by her side as she was still slipping her purse over her shoulders, his gentle touch surprising her, as she took his hand for that of one of the all too numerous bag-snatchers that worked this part of the city.

Yet looking up, she found herself swept away by a dream standing before her under the gentle Rio sunshine. He was taller, close to six feet in height, his skin the colour of honey, and he possessed a warm smile. He wore no shirt, his magnificently sculptured body glistening from a mixture of sweat and fresh sea spray. He was clothed in a pair of light white cotton trousers, and adorning his feet were a pair of fashionable leather sandals, lightly covered with a dusting of caramel sand from *Copacabana* Beach.

"How are you?" His voice deep and sensual, like sea on sand.

"Ahh, I'm very good! Umm…ahhh…who are you?" She stuttered.

"I'm who you're looking for, that's who I am."

"Ah I'm not looking for anyone, I'm just here for a walk…that's all…nothing else."

"Such a beautiful lady like yourself, all alone on a perfect day like this. At least do me the pleasure of accompanying you on your walk. No harm in getting to know a stranger?"

Isabella was mesmerized, struck by the beauty of the man before her, his determination to charm, the way he smiled, the gentle sway of his hips as he walked beside her. Swooning, dreaming, she tossed aside reason and accepted his offer, allowing him to fall into step at her side.

They made a magnificent sight walking alongside the seaside, the gentle midday breeze, the cries of children, the sounds of the seagulls and the waves. Fading beauty rejuvenated by handsomely debonair youth.

That was their first seaside walk; an awkward yet seductive stroll down alongside magnificent *Copacabana* Beach, under the shadows of *Corcovado*, amongst the riches of the city. She was seduced; charmed by a man she had known only in her dreams.

In the days that followed she and Chico met again for long walks, stopping to kiss each other tenderly along the seaside, caught up in the beginnings of a romance. Passion discovered, they soon began ending their strolls with passionate encounters at the most magnificent of the city's seaside motels, spending whole afternoons together.

Isabella knew her behaviour was irresponsible; however, she stopped caring as her abandon destroyed reason, forgetting her responsibilities or concern for what would happen should her husband discover her secret. She knew that should her affair ever be uncovered it would certainly tear her family apart, destroying her marriage to Carlos. Yet she was tired and frustrated with her lot, and no amount of guilt could force her to surrender something she had dreamed of for so long.

Her husband remained oblivious to what was going on, and it seemed as though she would be able to maintain her private life. Chico respected her privacy, never phoning her, and never questioning her if she was unable to join him at their designated meeting place in *Botafogo Bay*. Whenever she did not show he would knowingly understand she had been caught up in an engagement with her husband or one of her daughters. Isabella in turn respected Chico's privacy. She never asked him what he did for work, she never intruded in his private life, and she never voiced concern if he failed to show for one of their secretive meetings.

Their affair followed its adventuresome path, with each of them taking more and more risks as they fell further in love. At times Isabella returned home barely a few minutes before her husband, rushing in through the door just before the familiar De Silva limousine pulled into the parking space in front of the house. With her clothes changed in time, there was barely a moment for inventing excuses to satisfy him as to why dinner was late. Unbeknownst to Carlos, Isabella's excuses of doctor appointments or late walks were simply a screen of lies covering for days of steamy passionate love in expensive luxury hotels in *Botafogo* with Chico.

Isabella often wondered where Chico was able to find the money to pay for such quarters, since he rarely seemed to have to work; however, respecting their unwritten code, she never breached the subject.

Their unwritten code - it was perhaps for that reason Chico was so comfortable with her: he could be himself without having to answer any intrusive questions. Regardless of the reasons, Isabella felt like a beautiful and glamorous princess with him, revelling in the gifts he brought for her to wear on their wild afternoons of lovemaking. There were silk dresses, hats, rings, jewellery, and fine foods. It saddened her though that she was not able to bring their relationship into the open, that she could never wander Rio de Janeiro with Chico in tow and dressed in all their finery.

Then as suddenly as it began, it ended.

After six months of passion Chico suddenly vanished, not appearing for several weeks at their regular meetings on the seaside. At first Isabella attributed this to work her lover had been called in to do; however, eventually she came to realize that he had perhaps decided to end their relationship without any form of communication.

By July she felt more and more frustrated, not having seen or heard from him in nearly a month. At home she was unable to control her emotions, at times lashing out at her perplexed husband, and then refusing to explain her unusual behaviour. Her sexual frustration deepened as weeks of unsatisfied desires began to wear her down, driving her towards insanity. Eventually, realizing that something was terribly wrong, she elected to go to the police, hoping in some way they would be able to help track down her missing man.

One morning, after waiting for her husband to leave the house for his usual day of work driving Mr. De Silva, she hurriedly dressed and rushed out onto the damp rainy streets of Rio, not bothering to clean up the mess left behind by her daughters as they left for school earlier that morning. Once at the street corner, she flagged a bus heading for the city centre, and took a seat just behind the conductor's turnstile.

The bus ride was typically arduous, the city traffic blocking the streets into a congested crawl that had her wondering if she would be able to get to and from the station before her husband returned. After all, there was simply no idea of knowing how long it would take at the police station. The bus was hot and stuffy, sweaty hands clung to bus poles, dreary faces stared aimlessly under armpits at the rain that poured down in sheets upon the cars outside.

Isabella felt helpless, cloistered, trapped, without a sense of direction or a way out of an existence that had for years led nowhere and was now once and for all closing in on her. She sat there, thankful for having a seat, her mind wondering as she studied the faces of others, others, so many others. Were their lives any better than hers? Had things just somehow worked out for them in a way that it had not for her?

How could she know? The dreary faces and the sticky heat acting as grey screen of disconnect.

She arrived at Rio de Janeiro's gigantic federal police station, an austere grey building trapped between the city's elevated portside freeway on one side, and the filth of some of the worst parts of the city centre on the other. At the entrance there were the usual collection of homeless people, prostitutes, and tired looking police officers who seemed to have nothing better to do than watch the sheets of tropical rain pour down on the uneven streets that crisscrossed the plaza in front of the station.

Inside the air was heavy, laden with the sweet smell of unwashed floors and human sweat. The main hall was crowded and rather small; grey cement covered with a soggy carpet and people milling about with no apparent purpose. Trying to avoid the crowds, she looked for what seemed to be the right direction and followed a series of signs that directed her through winding hallways and up a plain cement staircase to the second floor. At the landing, she caught the eye of a blank looking staff sergeant, who mechanically directed her through a glass door that led to a general waiting room.

The room inside was humid and excessively hot, the walls covered in a fine layer of condensation and grime that seemed to slide ever imperceptibly down towards the floor. Another attendant instructed her to take a number and wait to be called.

She stood alone, clutching her purse, waiting for those before her to finish filing reports with the officers behind the counter. Once her number was called she walked forward, to tell her story. She had already planned in her mind what she would tell the police. When the questions came she spilled out her well-prepared account to the officer in front of her, showing no hesitation or uncertainty. Her story was plausible, that she had known Chico from frequent seaside conversations at a juice stand in *Copacabana*, and that one day he had disappeared without a trace. She said that after a month of unexplained absences she felt somewhat perturbed at his disappearance and felt compelled to find out, if possible, as to what had happened to him.

The officer showed no sign of emotion, requesting she fill out a series of forms explaining as much as she could about Chico, her relationship to him, and any other details she could think of. As she filled out the papers in the unbearable heat of the room she became aware of subtle details that initially had eluded her. The young officer serving her had an adolescent face; his skin still covered with the signs of youth, including fresh acne intermingled with the fine lines of an emerging beard. She also became aware that he was studying her as she filled out the forms, his eyes drifting over her arms, studying her fingers and the absence of a wedding ring.

Isabella felt awkward, as if the young man could see not only through her story, but also through her fine cotton dress to the skin below. Shaking ever so gently she hurriedly finished her report, sliding it over the desk to the young officer. He took the forms, letting his hand slide gently over hers. Isabella jumped, the young man panicked, looking up to see if any of his colleagues had seen, yet no one had noticed, all too entranced by the boredom of the day.

Leaving the police station she rushed across the square, dodging the puddles, looking about for an available taxi to whisk her away from the misery that surrounded that station. The streets were slippery, mixed with rain, refuse, and grease leaked from parked cars. Her shoes were not made for the conditions, and in her rush she missed her step and slipped on a loose stone, tumbling forwards into one of the many filthy puddles that littered the street side. Soaking wet, the front of her dress covered in splotches of mud, she slipped and struggled to feet, barely even noticed by the passing traffic that splashed by under the unrelenting tropical rain.

Days passed without any news. Her bruises faded, but her melancholy did not. She grew increasingly restless, trapped under the rain that poured from the sky day after day. She drifted in and out of reality, spending days sitting silently at home, hoping Chico would somehow magically appear, just as he had done those many months ago on that perfect day at the seaside.

Her husband appeared to not even notice her changes in mood, preferring to bury himself in the morning paper. Every morning was as silent as the one before, at times punctuated with a crisp comment about breakfast not being up to standard, lacking something, usually fruit, which she had stopped buying because the fruit market was too much to bear. Too much to bear as she feared running into one of the wives of her husband's friends – overbearingly curious women who thrived off the gossip and misery of others.

Her daughters may have observed how miserable their mother had become; however, if they did they made no mention of it. Indeed they seemed more preoccupied with the approaching school exams and the possibilities academic success would bring – better jobs, opportunities to travel abroad and learn English. Yes, her eldest daughter constantly spoke about how she wanted to go to London to study and learn English.

Then one Monday morning the news did come, in the form of two policemen who arrived at her doorstep several weeks later. Luckily, the house was empty, her husband and daughters having left a half an hour earlier. She invited them in, petrified that curious neighbours might notice them, starting a neighbourhood rumour. The police informed her brusquely that Chico had been killed in *a favela* during a shoot-out with security forces. Apparently Chico was a member of a drug ring caught in a battle for control of drug money in the southern part of the city, and an anonymous tip to the police had given his whereabouts.

Isabella was dumbstruck. How had it been that the man she had shared such intimacy with was some sort of mastermind criminal, whose dubious distinction was his entrepreneurial mastery in the world of cocaine, heroine, and narcotics? In an instant she understood how her lover had been able to pay for their lavish meetings and the mountains of gifts. Isabella felt dirty, used, and at the same time terribly scared of what she had just found out.

Holding back tears, she stared at the officers as they told her the story, listening to the details they were able to provide. Rather than make the meeting excessively complicated, fearing she may be dragged into something beyond her control that may endanger her family, she politely ended the conversation, saying there was nothing more she needed to know.

Nonetheless, they had questions of their own, wanting to know more about her interest in Chico. She explained she had known him simply through regular conversations down at the seaside where she liked to go and sip coco water while watching the surfers at her favourite stand. The policemen smiled, understanding the urges of an ordinary housewife, accepting her answer and obviously too disinterested to take the matter any further.

The news left Isabella with a sense of closure, knowing the mystery had been solved; however, learning her lover was no more was like a weight of sadness dropped on her chest. She knew that with his death her odds of ever again being intimate with a man were highly improbable. She sensed her destiny was now decided, that with the passing of the coming years she would grow old and tired alongside her ordinary husband.

In the weeks that followed she lay in the shadows of the night in bed beside her husband, tears flowing silently down her cheeks as she cried both for the death of a man she had barely known, and in humiliation for the adultery she had not only committed but that she profoundly needed.

Yet unaware to Isabella, her brush with adventure had not ended. It was simply beginning. A twisted web was waiting in the shadows, preparing to drag her and her family down into ruin. Several months after discovering the fate of her former lover, her eldest daughter, Julia Varas, disappeared off the campus of her university in *Urca*, the victim of a horrific gunpoint kidnapping in front of her classmates.

Chapter III

Faustino and Chico

Rio de Janeiro's *favelas*, as the city's hilltop slums were known, were territories of misery, shantytowns in once pristine rainforest born from squatters who had settled them many generations ago. Those original settlements had now ballooned to a point where they now housed close to half of Rio de Janeiro's population – millions of people outside of the socio-economic system, trapped in hilltop labyrinths wrought with rampant crime and unemployment, run by drug lords and not the police.

Favela life was so totally different from the universe below – a land of mystery often tucked away in the grey blanket of clouds and tropical mist that covered Rio de Janeiro for weeks at a time. Unlike the madness of the city streets below, where decades of population growth had transformed once quaint *Copacabana*, *Leme*, and *Botafogo* into a hell holes of traffic congestion, noise, and overcrowded apartments; the *favelas* in the sky were devoid of vehicles, their streets generally too narrow or too steep to permit the luxuries of motorized transport.

City and *Favela*: two solitudes.

The rich from below never ventured into the clouds above, while the poor from above refrained from disclosing any reference to where they came from. The silent rules between Rio's residents were quietly enforced through fear: fear of the police, fear of reprisals, fear of violence, and fear of the drug lords.

One of those drug lords was Chico Grande. He ran an established drug ring on the twisting and winding streets of a bedevilled shantytown *favela* hanging above the flashiest and wealthiest of Rio de Janeiro neighbourhoods. Chico's banda controlled a significant share of the massive local drug market, selling to the muscled middle and upper class of the city's elite, all of whom had an insatiable desire to shoot up on heroine, or sniff down some of the sharpest cocaine on the continent.

Born to a large lower class family, Chico had found his own way, moving out of home and seeking the support and sense of belonging that came with joining a drug ring. At a very young age he was already managing the distribution of small quantities of drugs and activities of some of the younger prostitutes working on *Avendida Atlantica.* His early success and survival instincts caught the attention of various influential players, and eventually he began moving up the ranks of the *Favela* drug trade staking his own turf, building his own dealer networks.

Before even leaving adolescence, Chico had surrounded himself with a close group of loyal partners who recognized his ability as a leader, and who knew the taste and smell of drug money. Some of his partners were simple *favelinhos* (inhabitants of the *favela*s), while others were powerful sources of money and weaponry from outside of the slums. Those powerful sources had no identity, and spoke only with Chico. They wanted no blood on their names - they simply sought access to the lucrative drug business and the political power it wielded.

As Chico liked to say, "Everything is interconnected: the politicians may say they want us out of the city; however, without us they are nothing. We are the force that gets them elected. Without our cooperation the slums would turn on them. The same can be said for the rich - they need us because we police the poor; we do the dirty work that the police could never hope to do."

Policing was exactly what Chico's gang did. They maintained a tense, but peaceful situation on their turf, breaking the silence only when neighbouring drug gangs tried to challenge territories and steal business, or when the Federal Police swept in on helicopters loaded with semi-automatic rifles and hand grenades. The police raids were usually folly: staged during periods of political importance, when the arms of the law would try to demonstrate their commitment to keeping the city safe. Blood baths, they achieved little, other than disrupting the equilibrium between drug cartels, and encouraging rearmament amongst the warring parties.

Supporting his business activities, Chico had various "players" – boys who he recruited off the street to work closely with him in his ventures. Many of them came and went, often falling prey to drug addiction or being caught by the police or rival gangs. Some survived, and as they grew older, became important well-rewarded allies in his quest to control the city's drug supply. Out of those few survivors an even smaller select few were able to get close to Chico, becoming like brothers over the years.

Of all of the survivors in his inner circle of brothers, his closest confidant was a tall mysterious young man by the name of Faustino. He had met Faustino at a party in *Santa Teresa* some years earlier. The younger man sweeping him off his feet as they engaged in conversation at the bar table, shouting and laughing over the cacophony of samba and funk, blasting from the dozens of bars lining the street.

Faustino, ah Faustino. When Chico met him, the boy was a penniless street kid struggling to survive. In fact he worked wherever he could, kickboxing for money in local contests, mingling with foreign tourists on the beach, handing out pamphlets on street corners, or if things got really bad, swiping the odd purse or two from defenceless old ladies in *Botafogo* and *Copacabana.*

Child of a tragic youth, Faustino had been born into utter poverty, the unwanted result of a foreign tourist who had raped his mother during her days as a prostitute. As Chico discovered, Faustino knew little about his mother, other than that the woman had been an alcoholic, who had died from a drug overdose, leaving him to be raised in a Christian orphanage in Rio de Janeiro's largest hilltop slum: *Rocinha.*

An only child, with no family, no friends, no one to look up to - his years at *Rochina* Missionary Orphanage did nothing to abate the anger and frustration of being an unloved child. By the age of ten Faustino had lived and survived more from being alone on the winding alleys of *Rocinha*, than most people more than twice his age living in the luxury apartments down in the city.

As a child, Faustino used cigarettes and marijuana as an escape from the misery of his existence in the slums, discovering the drugs after other children in the orphanage introduced him to the wonders of being high. Drugs were a problem throughout the *favela*s, but the orphanages were some of the worst places, providing ample recruiting grounds for future drug runners. Those children already in the trade knew that getting younger boys like Faustino addicted meant potential new recruits in the powerful game of drug running in Rio de Janeiro.

The missionaries running the orphanage were aware of the situation; however, their numbers were too small to save every child. All they could do was warn him and the other boys of the dangers of tobacco and marijuana: asthma, asphyxiation, lung cancer, brain damage, and that the soft drugs peddled to them were a slippery slope to harder addictions and a future dependency on the drug trade to sustain those needs.

Yet for Faustino, the hours of peace afforded from the mellowing combination of tobacco and marijuana were too much to pass on, besides, the missionaries seemed to turn a blind eye to his habits as long as he kept attending the mandatory daily church sermons.

Then suddenly the addiction ended - a violent asthma attack from a bad trip left him gasping for air and nearly dead in a filthy alleyway behind the orphanage.

Dead he would have been had he not been found by one of those same missionaries that ran his orphanage. They rushed him to a clinic, where he was given oxygen and a vital dose from an inhaler that opened his airway, allowing him to breath.

Alive, Faustino found himself forever indebted to the missionary who had saved him, and under the man's guidance he turned his energy to religion, convinced that the Lord had saved him from death to prepare him for some other greater purpose beyond the misery of life in the slums. Prayer became an important part of his life – and in the contradictions of the years ahead, no matter what the challenges, he never missed a day in Church, even if it met a quick few minutes of silent prayer in the late afternoon.

To escape the dangers of being lured back to drugs, Faustino began spending more time outside of the *favela*, wandering down to the seaside in *Ipanéma* and *Copacabana* - sea, smiling faces, and clean ocean air substituting the escape that drugs had once provided.

At the seaside he also made new friends, meeting various interesting characters at *Ipanéma* beach, a vast number of them single older men visiting Rio de Janeiro from places he had only vaguely heard of – Berlin, New Jersey, Toronto, Milan. It was all very new to him, glamorous and easy –

something he so desperately needed as an escape from the misery of the *favela.*

In the space of a few days, the experienced *gogo* boys working the beach introduced him to a small network of people, finally matching him with a tall athletic German tourist from West Berlin, who was on his third visit to "*Cidade Maravilhosa*"

Herman, as he was known, was a wealthy interior designer, with an affinity for youth – something that he could not entertain in his native Germany. He and Faustino soon became quite close, and Herman began to introduce Faustino to a new world of martial arts and weight training– two activities that Herman had practiced for many years and were an important part of his life. He offered Faustino, in exchange for his companionship, access to training at the city's top martial arts and fitness centre, where Herman enjoyed practicing during his visits to Rio de Janeiro. As Herman said, "*Karaté* will get you fit and off the street. It will also work you mind, making you smarter and stronger."

The man was an experienced practitioner, who saw much potential in Faustino's long lanky frame. Under his watchful eye, Faustino demonstrated a natural ability for the sport, and after some arm-twisting, the owner of the gym and dojo offered him free training in exchange for sharing winnings at future kickboxing competitions.

Faustino took quickly to the two sports, and it soon became evident that he was blessed with a natural athletic ability vastly superior to most other people. His body began to fill out, and the reach of his powerful long frame meant that most of his foes never even made contact, instead falling prey to blow after blow from his long legs and arms. Indeed he was formidable in kickboxing competitions, defeating opponents in age and weight classes beyond his own.

As he grew older, his relationship with Herman also evolved, as Faustino grew increasingly attached to his German big brother who promised him possibilities of a new life in a land far away from the misery of the slums of Rio de Janeiro. Then one day, towards the end of yet another visit to Rio de Janeiro, Herman announced to him that he would never be returning to Rio de Janeiro, that he had finally met a partner in Berlin who saw no interest in visiting Brazil, preferring the comforts and security of Europe. The last time they saw each other was on Faustino's eighteenth birthday, at a fancy restaurant where they were supposed to have been celebrating his transformation to adulthood, but instead were acknowledging the end of something that realistically had no future. Faustino was devastated - more than just a boyfriend who one day promised him a better life than the slums of Rio, Herman had become the father he had never known.

The loss of his mentor set Faustino adrift. He spent more time in Central Rio de Janeiro, venturing to parties where hard drugs were common, and where there were greater chances of meeting other men who shared his desires. At those parties Faustino rarely passed unnoticed - in addition to being physically imposing, he was remarkably beautiful, with a pale white complexion derived from his mixed European roots, and a dazzling mop of fiery red hair covering his brilliant blue eyes. He became known as "*Gringo Brasileiro*" - the beautiful Brazilian boy that looked like a foreigner.

Chico first spotted Faustino at a crowded street-side bar in *Lapa* - the younger man's brilliant red hair making him stand out amongst the revellers. Energized by the cocaine racing through his veins, Chico crossed the street, pushing through the crowds to move carefully beside the taller younger man. After a moment of hesitation, he abruptly uttered, "*Oi tudo bem cara? Esta sozinho?* How you doing guy? You alone?"

Faustino was clearly taken by surprise – transfixed under the penetrating gaze of the shorter athletic man standing beside him at the bar. Caught staring, Faustino had no way to dismiss the man's presence, and was forced to acknowledge with a, "*Tudo bem, estou sozinho.* Everything's cool, I'm alone."

Chico seized on the opening, offering to buy a round of drinks and introducing himself, "*Sou Chico do Rio,* I'm Chico from Rio."

Faustino answered, "*Faustino…me pega uma cerveja ta.* A beer okay."

Alcohol has a strange way of lifting inhibitions, allowing perfect strangers to communicate when otherwise they would have exchanged no more than a nod or a hello. As the evening passed, the two found themselves entwined in passionate discussion as Faustino spilled out his love for kickboxing and weights to Chico, expressing his hopes of one day becoming a champion, and maybe even winning a state title.

Chico listened, smiling, occasionally touching the younger man on the shoulder or the back, letting his hand stay just a bit longer and stray just a bit further than what would have normally been considered acceptable. Faustino showed no objection: his brain growing cloudier with each new glass of alcohol, his shyness fading as he found himself swept further under the spell of the older man.

That they were attracted to each other was understood.

Before the night turned to dawn they had left the energy of *Santa Teresa*, wandering on foot down to the heart of *Lapa* to find a motel. It was a Friday night, and as usual *Lapa* was still on fire with energy, as thousands of sweaty and near-naked revellers filled the neighbourhood's dark and contorted cobbled streets, twisting and spinning to the sounds of whatever spilled from the noisy sidewalk bars and cafés.

To the sounds and energy outside their room on the street below, Faustino and Chico fell over each other in an erotic frenzy, engaging in a forbidden encounter, driven by their deepest sexual desires and the combination of alcohol and drugs coursing through their bodies. As they made love their sweat and tears soaked the sheets of the dingy motel room in *Lapa*, the only witnesses to their sin against God being the insects crawling on the ceiling above their bed.

That would not be their only encounter. Over the months ahead they arranged other secretive encounters at various locations in the city centre. They always avoided the shantytowns, since there they were least likely to be recognized by rival gangsters or the Federal Police.

Their late night trysts continued for months unabated, as Faustino found himself more and more obsessed with Chico. In the daytime, when he was working at the gym or kickboxing, he craved the presence of the older man, counting the minutes of the day before their next meeting. If they were unable to meet Faustino would become desperate, conjuring images of a Chico in trouble, hurt, or worse: cheating with someone else.

One night, after months of similarly intense meetings, their ritual of passionate encounters was rudely interrupted.

The door of their motel room was kicked open and two large black men walked in sporting shotguns. They were rival hit men who had tracked Chico to the motel, somehow succeeding in deciphering his combinations of taxis and buses designed to throw off anyone who may be following.

The invaders stood beside the broken door, laughing as Chico and Faustino tried to loosen each other from their sweaty bond. Then using their guns, they forced the two men to stand naked before them with their hands in the air. The humiliation was unbearable, and if it were not for weapons pointed their way, Faustino would have sprung upon them in fury.

Yet the humiliation did not last long, as in a maddening instant Chico threw himself across the room, taking one of the burly guards down before he was able to fire his weapon, using him as a shield while the other fired bullets into his partner's stomach. Faustino dropped to the ground, sweating and cursing as the crazy spectacle unfurled before him, his years of weight training and martial arts failing him as his nerves frayed. The one man was clearly dead, blood pouring from his bullet-laden gut, while the other swore loudly, his head in a chokehold, trying to free himself from Chico and reload his rifle at the same time.

It seemed an eternity, but in fact it was within a few minutes that they were outside, tearing through the revelling crowds of another noisy rain-soaked street in *Lapa*, as they left the two bodies and the blood splattered room behind them. The two spent the night curled beside each other in a ditch in *Flamengo* Park, deciding that to return to the slums in their current state would be suicide. In the morning they split up - Chico returning to his territory, leaving Faustino to wander in exhaustion and bewilderment on *Avendida Atlântica* in *Copacabana*, before seeking solace and God in the familiarity of his favourite church, located in *Ipanéma*.

It was Faustino's first real contact with the icy hand of death since his asthma attack, and from that moment on he was all the more obsessed with the man that had saved him from near death. At that point he knew he would give everything to be with Chico, including his life.

Their relationship now cemented through their common experience, in the months ahead Chico began to entrust Faustino with secrets that very few ever heard. Obsession and a newly found addiction to cocaine, combined with the possibility of riches clouded Faustino's judgement, and in the ensuing months he allowed Chico to bring him into the drug ring, making him responsible for a fair share of the business, including meeting with important clients from the wealthy elite in *Botafogo, Ipanéma*, and *Copacabana.*

Obsession ruins lives, it tears people apart, making them irrational, and driving them to strike out and harm the ones they love and trust most. It was this obsession that resulted in Faustino discovering Chico's affairs with women. His spying led to him learning of Chico's charades in *Copacabana* with older women, how he charmed them and then loved them in secretive locations.

At first Faustino ignored Chico's daytime absences, understanding that unlike him, Chico held a profound interest for women that needed to be satisfied. Yet he soon realized that this interest was more profound than simple afternoon sex, that in fact his friend had become increasingly involved with a married woman from a middle class neighbourhood in *Tijuca.*

His discovery was too much to bear. In a state of drug induced fury, he decided if he could no longer have the man he obsessed after, it would be better to have him disappear forever.

In a matter of days Chico secretly planned his lover's killing. Realizing he could not involve anyone from his cartel – doing so could mean reprisals as well as questions about his relationship with Chico – he went outside of the *favelas* to find his assassin, dropping an anonymous tip with the

Federal Police as to the whereabouts of Chico and a supply of drugs and weapons their cartel had accumulated.

The tip was like magic. By the end of the day the news was in all the papers: Chico, one of Rio de Janiero's most wanted cartel leaders was dead, shot down with dozens of others in a police ambush in one of the *favelas* above Rio de Janeiro.

In the aftermath of Chico' death, Faustino drifted into a period of profound anguish. His moods swayed from pain and grief, to anger and rage. In his wretched state he realized the finality of his act: Chico was gone forever, victim of treachery, and the traitor had been him, Faustino.

"*Merda*, Chico, why did you cheat on me? If you had of remained faithful you would still have been alive today, and we still would have been together!"

His friends, of whom there were few, disappeared, fearing the ominously dark clouds beginning to swirl about the young man. Band members, who had for so long been loyal to both Chico and himself, decided to distance themselves. No one knew of Faustino's role in Chico's murder; however, they all feared a fiery revenge from the younger man, who obviously had held a special relationship with the dead drug king.

In the nights following his lover's death, a death he knew he was in large part responsible for, Faustino took to the streets of central Rio de Janeiro. In solitude he wandered, armed with his favourite pistol and a small bag of cocaine to satisfy his addiction and his need to escape from a painful and sombre reality. His wanderings took him beyond Rio's downtown *Centro* to the dark and dilapidated lower middle class neighbourhoods of *Sao Cristovao* and *Maracana*, which at night were nothing more than deserted streets and shuttered shops.

Central Rio de Janeiro was dangerous. Surrounded by a patchwork of slums and decaying middle class neighbourhoods, the centre was a far cry from the joy and privilege of the colourful neighbourhoods of *Ipaněma*, *Botafogo*, and *Leblon*. One could understand the sense of hopelessness permeating the air, millions of people trapped in a sea of grey cement, whose existences were just that: animals in dank cages peering out from shuttered windows and armed gates, into a dark and polluted night.

Rio de Janeiro's middle class neighbourhoods were not the middle class neighbourhoods of the West, as seen on television shows and movies played in the cinemas. There were no children riding about the streets on bicycles, or youngsters returning home on foot from a carefree night of parties. These neighbourhoods, like much of the Rio de Janeiro that was not fortunate enough to be inside gated communities, were buffer zones, protecting the rich from the poor, layers upon layers of concrete and human misery slaving away to support a system that was rotten to the core.

Faustino, despite his chosen path as a drug man and a murderer, knew just how power was played out in Rio de Janeiro. Street smart, he understood the fundamentals of Brazil's political system – how the rich used the middle class as a buffer to protect themselves from the poor, and that the politicians were in the game, accepting bribes to achieve personal enrichment at the expense of long term prosperity.

Faustino hated the system – he blamed its failure for the misery he lived in. If the politicians actually made the right decisions, the hard ones required to clean up the country's horrid bureaucratic mess and shut down the corruption, then the world of slums and violence would dissipate, the money going to the people who needed it, not those who languished in wealth and prosperity with their fortunes shipped abroad.

Yet as much as he hated the ruling class he realized they were of fundamental importance to the success of his own business. He had seen it with Chico, witnessing the secretive negotiations between gangsters and powerful political families to ensure a controlled peace. The drug bandits gained access to weapons to police their turf, while the political class got a tolerable level of violence and drug use that was constrained to the poorer neighbourhoods.

Over the nights of wandering the streets in solitude, Faustino gradually came to understand the opportunity that lay before him. Yes, he had lost Chico; however, his friend had left him a legacy, a chance to take control of the city's enormous drug trade and in turn create a fortune for himself. In the darkness, high on cocaine and with a pistol in hand, it dawned on him that the system, in its corrupt and bureaucratic way, really could work, but only if he learned to use it as it was designed to be used: through violence and manipulation.

His mourning passed, and out of the shadows of regret he set about fighting for a business he believed was rightfully his. Over the weeks ahead he began a brutal process of shoring up his power base, eliminating those around him whom he believed to be traitors to both him and Chico.

His fury was Rio de Janeiro's fear, as he began one of the city's bloodiest crackdowns against rivals and the police. Over the ensuing weeks he showed his mettle, demonstrating a ruthless side that astounded even him - organizing the killing of his deceitful lover had been one thing, but slaughtering men, women, and children to establish a new order was another. Faustino became a raging bull, showing no mercy for the slightest insubordination, yet rewarding loyalty abundantly.

His silent allies from the other side observed his progress in earnest, and as they saw him win more turf wars they became more numerous in their financial support. Secretly the political class and the business establishment appreciated the arrival of a new drug tycoon to take care of their "dirty work". It meant stability and certainty – something that had been absent with the power vacuum created with Chico's death.

For Faustino, having the rich onside meant less harassment from the police and more discreet money to fund the purchase of weapons and allies in the slums. His stake in the drug trade also grew as the sons and daughters of the middle and the upper classes turned to him for a secure and safe supply of drugs to satisfy their needs. With more drug money came more weapons and more political support. Faustino proved to be a mastermind bandit, emulating the trickery of his deceased friend, who had been a master at manipulating Rio de Janeiro's elite to get the weapons he needed.

The putsch in his *favela* complete, and his power base established, Faustino realized he needed a more secure supplier of arms to be able to protect himself from both the police and newer more powerful enemies in adjacent slums. He decided to turn to an old friend, one of Rio de Janeiro's leading kick boxers, and someone he had fought against many a times in the ring. The man was a formidable fighter, not tall, but incredibly talented, and one of the few that Faustino had ever lost to.

His name was Eduardo De Silva, the son of a wealthy Brazilian industrialist and real estate tycoon, and he had his fingers in every political party in the state. Eduardo De Silva respected Faustino, admiring the man's rise to the upper echelons of a merciless business, and respecting his capacity as a tactician in martial arts – a fighter who had beaten him on several occasions.

The two young men came from completely different social and economic classes – one from privilege and the other from poverty. However, joined in the vicious desire for power they realised together there was much they could achieve: Faustino offered safe and discreet access to drugs, while Eduardo offered money and supply lines to weapons

With their silent pact, over the months following Chico's death Faustino gradually became the leader of the drug trade across Rio de Janeiro's slums, he mercilessly sought out any resistance to his new reign, gunning down anyone who attempted to challenge his control of the trade. No longer was he known as "*Gringo Brasileiro*", instead his foes referred to him as "*Gringo Invencivel*" - Invincible because somehow he survived every attack on his life.

Rarely did Faustino and Eduardo meet, preferring to restrict their discussions to communications between drug runners or discreet conversations to mobile telephones. When they did meet it was for urgent matters, requiring direct communication. On those occasions Faustino and Eduardo took care to leave Rio de Janeiro, opting to meet either outside of the city, or, on several occasions, in adjacent states.

Their last meeting took place outside of Rio de Janeiro in *Punta del Este*, a luxurious holiday town three hours west of Montevideo in Uruguay. The two met discretely on a rented yacht, making sure no one would have access to their conversation, or to any record of their meeting.

Eduardo clearly stated what he wanted: continuity and stability in the drug trade, better access to drugs, and in return a commitment to providing weapons and political shelter crucial to Faustino's survival.

Yet there was more. Eduardo wanted one more thing from him, he wanted Faustino to finish off unfinished business, and eliminate Isabella Varas, the woman who had stolen Chico away from him.

Faustino was surprised, he had not revealed his affair with Chico to anyone, yet somehow, through means that Eduardo refused to reveal, he had found out about Faustino and Chico, and intended to use it to his advantage.

Eduardo's proposition was simple: Faustino would kidnap Isabella's daughter and hold her ransom, threatening to murder the girl and make public Isabella's secret affair with Chico. In order to save herself and her daughter, Isabella would be blackmailed into murdering Eduardo's brother David. If she failed to do so, her daughter would be killed and her secret exposed, ruining her family.

Eduardo finished his proposition by reminding Chico that if all were done as planned then his affair with Chico would be as good as forgotten, and his access to guns and funds would be assured for many years to come.

Chapter IV

David

David and João hurriedly gathered their things together for dinner. They were excited, especially David, since he had so much to tell his father.

"Arrh I can't find my new shoes!" cried David, "This is so frustrating, I bought them just yesterday! How could they have gone missing so fast?"

"João have you seen them? Please tell me you've seen them!"

"David, forget about the shoes, we're late and your father must be tired as hell having just come in from wherever he was. The last thing he's going to think about is whether his son has the latest pair of Armani shoes or not. I honestly think he's a hell of a lot more interested to hear about his favourite son's new job at the World Bank."

"Okay, fine, fine…Let's go, let's go!"

They were out of their apartment in no time, whisking quickly along the polished hall of their marbled apartment to the brass-adorned elevator with satin handles.

The drive from their apartment to his father's beachfront penthouse in *Ipanéma* was for the most part uneventful, as they idly listened to chatter on the radio about the country's upcoming national elections and the possibility of a Lula presidency.

The street corners and traffic lights were filled with the usual clusters of street kids and hawkers peddling whatever they could find to passing motorists – a sad reminder of a dysfunctional society where crime and suffering were everywhere.

Those tragic images were the reasons why David had been determined from a very young age to find solutions to the lack of political will that was responsible for the fate of so many young people. The images of starving girls and boys on street corners haunted him. How was it that a society could just leave these people out on the fringe with nothing? Why did the rich of Brazil, rather than reach out to the poor, prefer to fence themselves in behind walls? It was as if in doing so they could ignore the problem, sidestepping the necessary process of broad social and economic development.

David's research at the *Universidade Féderal do Rio de Janeiro* centred on the concepts of economic development as a means to achieve social stability and a just and economically prosperous society. His work was based on the premise that in any society, once riches were distributed more broadly, the basic institutions of justice, the rule of law, and education would quickly be adopted. Essentially by giving the poor access to the benefits of economic growth they in turn would begin to respect the country's institutions. These premises, taken together, would bolster economic growth as more people would have the income to participate in the economy, while more foreign investors would enter the economy, reassured by a decrease in violent crime.

Yet in Brazil, as in most emerging economies, individuals and corporations had no interest in educating the poor and giving them jobs. Doing so would be like throwing a bucket of water into an ocean: the benefits would be too diluted to make any difference. Thus rather than doing anything at a collective level, the upper strata of Brazil's society preferred to ignore the problem, electing to fence themselves in and manipulate the poor with the principles of populist politics.

David's views occasionally opposed those of his father's, who believed that even if the poor had the means to solve their problems through education, they would still continue to choose the path of crime and violence. This was because, as his father argued, the poor needed the rich political and business elite for guidance and governance, since the lower classes inherently lacked this ability. His father claimed that only through many generations of work would any member of the lower classes truly be able to rise to levels of responsibility and leadership.

David had learnt to avoid the topic with his father, knowing it to be the only issue that seemed to cause friction between the two. He valued his relationship with his father too much to have his social and political views come between them. The fact that he had so determinedly supported David during his coming out process, fighting David's mother over her unjustified action, which ultimately led to the end of their marriage, was for David a source of admiration. His father had his principles, both good and bad, he knew when to defend them, and for the most part he and David saw eye to eye on almost everything.

"Hello my boys! How are you? Come in come in! Dinner is already on the table. Maria, the boys have arrived, you can put the food out!" beamed Mr De Silva.

They were led out onto the penthouse patio overlooking *Ipanéma*. The view was breathtaking; there was no other word to describe it. From the immense patio one had a clear view across the *Ipanéma* beach scene, with its patterned side walks, its gigantic swaying palm trees, and the rich caramel coloured beach sand that swept out into the turquoise Atlantic. The only sounds, swept up to the balcony from below, were the cries of the late afternoon sunbathers as they enjoyed their last swim of the day and the squawks of gliding seagulls floating lazily in the wind.

A glass railing and a lush rooftop garden framed the patio, complete with tropical plants and a grassy lawn; there were also several granite water fountains that flowed into a magnificent swimming pool and adjoining hot tub.

"So boys, what next, what are the plans for now?" asked David's father as the three of them took their seats at the set table on the balcony.

Smiling at David, João spoke, "Well for now nothing has changed, really. We are still in our usual routine; however, the news over the past couple of days has certainly gotten us excited. Now that David will be able to finish earlier we should be able to quite easily be in New York by the end of the summer, which is perfect for us, since it means we'll miss the grey cold of a New Yorker winter - for one year at least!"

Luis smiled at his son-in-law and added, "True, there is nothing worse than New York, or North America for that matter, during the winter. My trip there this past week was just too awful. I still do not understand how those poor people are able to cope with such horrible weather…that cold, and then those summers, almost as hot as ours!"

"How was the trip papa? Were you able to solve the issues with the bankers as you had hoped?"

"Seems to be fine once again. They were worried that my purchase of two New York properties would affect my credit position in the United States. Basically I told them that if there was a problem I could simply bring more funds from Brazil. Hey I mean that's easy enough, I've already brought 300 million dollars out since January last year."

There was brief silence, as Luis realized the hypocrisy of his comment – was it not he who was the first to complain about the rich sending wealth abroad. He decided to change topics, electing to focus on the boys, and their upcoming move to America.

Dinner was delightful, as David's papa's most loyal of servants; his 60-year-old servant of thirty years drowned their palates in a magnificent medley of Brazilian flavours. They finished the meal inside over drinks and the live sounds of Bossa Nova, as João pulled one of Luis' guitars from the family recording room. João had a beautiful voice, his soft pale face and gentle brown eyes smiling poetically he sang and played.

David was in love, and had been since the day he had met João at a flirty social gathering for artists and musicians some six years ago. He had unwillingly gone with a group of friends to check out what seemed to be an interesting social crowd at a worthwhile presentation of *favela* art, produced by several up and coming artists from the slums. The night had started dull, with too much bad music and an excessive amount of attractive women who never stopped hounding David for a moment of his time. It was known by many of Rio's elite that David was the son of the city's richest real-estate tycoon, and obviously a worthy catch. Not only was he rich, he was also dashingly handsome, sporting his father's good looks, with a prominent jaw, a sharp nose, and brilliant turquoise eyes that literally had women swooning before him.

Yet David knew he was gay, and while he was not out to many, including his family, several of his close friends were aware of his tastes, and invariably it was one of them that would drag him out to those types of parties to meet potential boyfriends.

David had been the first to catch João's eye, and after about thirty minutes of circling around at the party, the two young men were finally able to connect in a quieter space. There was no doubt in either of their minds of their physical attraction towards one another; however, over the course of the evening they discovered a deep connection at an intellectual level. David learnt of João's studies in music and economics at *Pontifica Universidade Catolica*, one of Brazil's leading universities, as well as his own work in writing. João also came from a wealthy family, and his family was most supportive of his life style and his career objectives.

João discovered a young man with much promise. David was brilliant, demonstrating knowledge for the issues of the world well beyond his tender age of eighteen.

Their first night together passed too quickly, and it took several intrusions from their friends to finally wrest the two apart as the party began to close its doors. Yet their connection was made, and within several months the two were living together, David explaining his relationship as a university roommate, and João proudly introducing his partner to his supportive family as his first and only boyfriend.

David remembered his father's reaction to his request to share an apartment with João. Mr. Luis De Silva was initially most unsupportive; however, after some convincing agreed to put this new friend of David's under a full interrogation. That first meeting between João and Luis had been a stressful affair; however, in the end David's father liked João quite a bit, recognizing the boy's family from various important financial boards in Sao Paulo and Rio de Janeiro. His father had simply declared following the meeting, "The boy is of good stock, so your new living arrangements are approved."

David's mother had said nothing, as usual showing no interest in the activities of her son.

Now six years later the three of them were seated in Luis' living room listening to the sounds of a magnificent guitar as the *Ipanéma* sunset faded from fiery oranges to black, and the first stars began to appear in the sky.

João finished his playing, and Luis, after much applause, admitted his exhaustion and that it was time to call it a night. The boys bade farewell to their papa, and headed for the lift, returning to their car in the garage below.

None them knew it would be the last time the three of them would be together.

João awoke the following morning bathed in sweat, the air conditioning was out, and the flat was steaming hot, the bed sheets soaked with his and David's sweat. He stepped out of bed, walking naked from the bedroom to the living room, where he found a note on the kitchen counter.

"Hi my love! Hot today, I went to the supermarket to pick up some things and also see why the air conditioning is out again. I should be home at about 10:30. Love you!"

João looked at the clock in the kitchen. It was midday. Odd, David was never one to be late. João picked up one of the cell phones lying on the sofa and phoned his boyfriend's line. There was no answer, which was really strange, since in their six years together João could count on one hand the number of times that his partner did not answer the telephone.

João nearly had a heart attack as the house telephone sounded; he rushed over to the phone, answering it. "*Oi, quem fala?* Hello, who is it?"

"João Norton *por favor.*"

"*Falando, quem é*? Speaking, who is this?"

"Mr. Norton, this is the police…[silence]…We are sorry to inform you that your friend, Mr. David De Silva…[silence]…was hit by a car this morning, he was rushed to the hospital….ahhh….but didn't make it... We are very sorry, very sorry. We are desperately trying to reach his father, Mr De Silva, and only had your phone number on identification. Do you have a number where we…"

João was stunned, his body turned weak and he dropped the phone, erupting into uncontrollable shaking, eventually crashing to the floor as he hit his head on the side of the kitchen counter.

When he came to he found himself in a hospital room, under the expectative eyes of his mother and Luis De Silva. He felt weak, his head hurt, and he was covered in a layer of cold sweat.

"David, where is David? I want him here now, I need him here now!" he cried.

His mother rushed towards him, wrapping her arms around her distraught son's shoulder, his head covered in a layer of dressings. Mr. De Silva looked weak and uncertain of himself, not quite sure how to address the young man before him.

For the first time in his life Luis felt completely helpless. In all his years he had always been able to solve any problem that had come to face him, whether it had been toughened business adversaries, his wife in divorce courts, or his own personal ailments, he had never failed to defeat the challenger. Yet this time everything was different. In an instant his son had been stolen from him, and a wonderful young man, who had become so much of a part of his family, had been reduced to a tearful, defeated soul. Unable to cope with the enormity of his loss, Luis turned his head from João, and fled the room.

In an instant their worlds had been changed.

Fury

"Sir there is no doubt. Your son's death was not an accident. The police department has a confession from the woman who did it."

Stunned, Luis dropped the phone back onto its cradle, not even bothering to respond to the police officer on the other end of the line.

He sat staring in silence at the mug shots on his desk. The woman in the photo was no stranger; she was close to his family, an individual he had trusted for many years. Her name was Isabella Varas, the wife of Luis' driver, Carlos Varas.

Luis acted swiftly. Burning with fury, he fired his driver, swearing to the man that he and his family would lose everything for what Carlos' wife had done. Carlos did not even have a chance to explain, or even mention that his eldest daughter had vanished, victim of a mysterious kidnapping.

Once Carlos had been dismissed and escorted from the premises, Mr. De Silva then called the banks to pull all financial assistance from under the feet of the Varas family. In an instant they were left penniless, their home, income, and lives ruined.

Humiliation and Salvation

Humiliated, ruined, and defeated, Carlos wandered the streets of Rio de Janeiro in solitude, arriving home well after dark. The house was silent and all the lights were out. Pushed under his front door was a mysterious envelope, which he carried with him into the kitchen.

Seated at the kitchen table, he tore open the envelope, his hands shaking. The letter inside revealed the unimaginable: how for six months his wife had been meeting an infamous drug dealer by the name of Chico for frequent encounters in *Botafogo*. This while Carlos was at work, and his daughters were at school.

Carlos was stunned. Never would he have imagined that his wife would cheat on him. How could she have done such a thing, turning her back on her husband, her family, and the testimony of God? He sobbed, staring through tears at the note before him, his daughter still missing, his wife in prison for murder, his job and finances ruined, and his boss' son, dear David De Silva, a boy of such promise, murdered by his own Isabella.

There seemed after all nothing left to live for, all of his hopes and dreams dashed in one brutal moment. Carlos had no idea who was responsible for this misfortune. Whoever had engineered the plot to kidnap his daughter and use his wife to kill David, remained hidden in shadow.

The weeks passed, but the situation remained unchanged. Isabella Varas confessed her crime before the courts, saying she had been a victim of extortion, and given no option, had chosen to sacrifice herself and David De Silva to save her daughter. She claimed she had acted as any mother would have under the circumstances; however, when asked as to who had forced her hand, she was unable to say.

There remained no news of the whereabouts of the Varas daughter. Everyday that passed remained capped in a cloud of uncertainty. Unemployed and without the financial means to sustain his family, the Varas' were quickly forced to sell their home, moving back to a small crowded flat in *Copacabana.* The move had happened so quickly; however, Carlos saw no other option, if he wanted to be able to put food on the table and continue to send his two other daughters to good schools, he would need the capital from the old family home. His daughters spoke little of the tragedy that had befallen their household, returning late from school and leaving in the morning before their father awoke.

Finally, after nearly three months of frustration, Julia Varas' body was found washed up beside the canal in *Leblon.* Her corpse was in a gruesome state; however, DNA testing was able to confirm her identity. Stunned and in a state of shock, Carlos went to the prison that held his wife, not only to tell her the news, but also to curse her for the death of his daughter and the misery that had befallen them.

His condemned wife was not the woman he remembered. It was the first time seeing her in many weeks since the brief trial, and she was frail, her hair grey and cut short, like a boy's. She had no smile, and her now thin face was covered with dark patches, her arms marked with cuts and bruises. She uttered not a single word as Carlos swore at her, staring unnervingly from behind the chicken wire fence at the man that had once been her husband. Carlos left the place in frustration, swearing he would never return to see that woman again.

His wife was found dead the following day, hanging from a makeshift lasso made from her bed sheets. In death she had an air of tranquillity – her face a mixture of blue and white blotches as she swung serenely back and forth in her musky cell. As is custom in Brazil, her body was delivered to the city morgue in central Rio for examination. There was no investigation into the cause of her death, the prison guards declaring that it was suicide. Three days after her autopsy was completed she was buried in a quiet and simple ceremony at a small cemetery on the outskirts of Rio de Janeiro. The only people to attend were her parents and her two remaining daughters.

Carlos gradually began a descent into a world of lunacy. His family no longer attended church, as his daughters took to caring for their own needs, living their own lives in the city. Carlos sought no work, and the remaining funds from the sale of their house were eaten away as he invested his assets in the consumption of alcohol to deal with his loss. In the day he spent his time wandering the streets, unshaven and dishevelled, his clothes wrinkled and dirty - proof of a man who had never really known how to care for himself.

The church and God drifted from his mind as he discovered an inner world of solitude that consisted principally of garbled conversations with his deceased wife and his murdered daughter. At night his two children would lie in bed, listening to their father cry out, "Isabella, Isabella, you are so beautiful, come to me here my love!"

Their father's deranged behaviour led to his two daughters suddenly moving out. They announced their decision to their father on a rainy Sunday morning, a day that used to be reserved for church, when the whole family would dress in their finest outfits. The girls declared that living with their father was not conducive to their academic obligations and that since Monica, his second daughter, had been accepted to the state funded university in Sao Paulo, they had decided to move to Sao Paulo where they would also be nearer their grandparents. Monica had also found a job, and along with their maternal grandparent's help they would be able to pay for Alicia's school and their living costs without his support.

Carlos had nothing to say as he watched them spend the day furiously packing. The following morning Monica's boyfriend and Carlos' in-laws arrived to load everything into small white van. There were no greetings exchanged, neither any goodbyes, and by sunset the apartment in *Copacabana* was all but empty, apart from a few items in the kitchen and some loose decaying furniture and family pictures.

"Jesus Mary what have I become? Lord, so hard I have worked to be your humble servant and now all I have is this. Why, why me? How could such a simple and good man be served such grief and sorrow in what should be the height of his moment on this earth? God save me, I beg you please!" cried Carlos into the darkness of his barren flat.

The next morning, as if his words had been heard, amongst the piles of Christmas bills and junk mail was another unmarked letter addressed with his name. Carlos took it to the kitchen and sat down to read the pages contained within. It was cold and clear, explaining the uncertainty of his wife's affair with a man Carlos had never known, whilst also shedding clear light on another man, a man who had not only murdered his daughter, but had also dragged the De Silva and the Varas families into ruins.

As he read, Carlos learnt more of his wife's affair of nearly six months, her frequent meetings with Chico at various locations on the seaside in *Botafogo* for lusty afternoons of secretive sex, while Carlos was at work and his daughters at school. The man, known as Chico Grande, had a dubious past as a powerful drug baron in the Rio de Janeiro underworld. Chico, in addition to his drug dealings, was also known for his sexual tastes, which included amongst them young men. Over the years he had developed a trail of male lovers, adding to the various women that he took to seducing along the streets of Rio de Janeiro. He had ultimately fallen in love with a young man by the name of Faustino, some insignificant hoodlum who had been swept up by Chico, becoming not only his long time lover, but also his right hand man in the drug trade.

The letter went on to explain that Faustino had eventually learnt of his lover's unfaithfulness and his affair with Carlos' wife Isabella. He had decided to follow the two for some time, wanting to determine the level of intimacy they had begun to build. Seeing that Isabella had begun to steal Chico away from him, Faustino finally engineered the kidnapping of the Varas' oldest daughter, using her as a tool of extortion to get Isabella to not only murder the son of Rio's greatest family, but also in doing so ruin the family and the woman who had taken Faustino's lover away.

As for Chico, Faustino had him eliminated by paying off the Federal Police as to Chico's whereabouts. The police had acted on the anonymous tip, ambushing the bandit on a hilltop slum just near *Leme.* In customary fashion Chico had attempted to gun himself out of the assault, but superior police preparedness and firepower overwhelmed him, and after thirty minutes Chico and his small posse were dead. The story was of no surprise to Carlos, since it had been all over Rio de Janeiro's press. It had been considered the greatest police coup of the year, since not only did the tip result in the elimination of one of the city's most feared mob leaders, but it also led to the capture of a significant stash of firearms and drugs.

Carlos stared at the letter in silence, tears rolling down his cheeks, wetting his unshaven face. He had found his answer; redemption was near at last after so much waiting.

On a sunny Wednesday morning Carlos left the house clean-shaven, sporting a brilliantly pressed suite and freshly polished shoes. He carried his leather briefcase in one hand and his umbrella in the other, looking like any other middle-class Carioca on his way to work. Carlos caught the Metro-bus to *Ipanéma*, exiting at *Vinicius de Moraes.* He then walked quickly up the street, arriving in time for the morning services at *Ipanéma*'s largest Evangelical Church. There were quite a few people, not unusual given that it was just after Christmas.

Carlos sat down at the rear of the church, listening to the hymns that for so long had been an important part of his family's existence. As he sat there he found himself humming along, mumbling the words, as a steady stream of tears began to softly flow down his face.

The minister cried out, "The people will be free to find their hearts if they trust in God. The people will be free if they let God enter them, and through them God will show the way. A miracle will happen when the words of the Lord are heeded by the man that listens!"

"Open your eyes and find God! Show no fear, for God is in us all!"

Carlos opened his briefcase and pulled out the pistol he had carefully loaded and polished that morning. He stepped into the aisle and walked four pews down until he saw the tall redheaded man in the photo that had come with the mysterious letter. He pulled the gun from his pocket, and without the slightest hesitation shot the man five times before firing the remaining bullet into his own skull.

In an instant Carlos found God, taking Faustino with him.

Chapter V

Eduardo

A high-pitched noise, ringing over and over again pulled him out of deep sleep and into the present. Instinctively his hand reached for the cordless telephone behind his bed.

"*Oi*…" he mumbled.

"Eduardo it's your mother. Turn on your television."

"*Oi* mama, sorry I was just asleep, late night you know..."

Grasping the phone Eduardo reached over for the television remote, turning on the large flat-screen television perched over his dresser. Quickly flipping the channels through the usual afternoon soaps he landed on number eight, *Globo News*. The station was alive with chatter, a sexy long-legged female reporter, whom he recognized from somewhere, was standing in front of a church.

Eduardo smiled, it was the church in *Ipanéma*, the one Faustino attended everyday, and the place that Eduardo had told Carlos Varas to go to in the carefully scripted letter his mother had prepared several days earlier.

"You have it on now?" his mother asked.

"Yes, yes I do, on *Globo News*. It's some blond bitch reporting in front of the church in *Ipanéma*. She's saying there was a shooting…two deaths…something to that effect."

"Yes two died, tragic isn't it. Appears that one of them was a drug dealer and the other your father's former chauffeur. I should call your father, see if he knows about the news, and how he's doing."

"Yes mama, good idea to see how the old man is doing. Love you!"

"Love you too," as the phone went silent.

Eduardo stared at the television for some time. There were estranged people everywhere, people crying, and several women covered in blood lay on the sidewalk, being attended to by paramedics.

The news reporter babbled on and on, "It appears the man, whose identity continues to remain unknown, walked in with a revolver and just began shooting madly. He took his life after killing another man at the front…"

"Melissa, can you tell us anything about the victim, any ideas or information as to his identity?

"Alessandro, at the moment no knows seems to know much at all. There are even conflicting accounts of exactly what happened in there, all we know is that two people are confirmed dead and many others are in a continued state of shock…"

The chatter between the anchorman and the long-legged reporter continued on pointlessly, and after a few minutes Eduardo grew bored of what they had to say, stepping from the bed, the silk sheets sliding off his smooth, muscular, olive-skinned body.

Eduardo walked naked into the bathroom, his step lighter than usual, his splendid twenty four-year-old athletic frame reflecting in the mirror along the wall. He admired himself, playing with his messy hair and flexing his muscles, aroused by his reflection – an image of human perfection.

He turned on the tap, splashing water on his face and then reached for his toothbrush, drowning it in mint toothpaste. As he brushed his teeth he walked slowly back and forth. He gazed at himself, struck by his own beauty. He wasn't tall, only about 5'8", but he had a powerful muscular frame built up over years of martial arts and weight training. His short black hair, accentuated his brilliant green eyes, inherited from his mother.

"Yeah," he murmured, "I am so hot. No wonder every woman wants me."

He began playing with his genitals, stroking his penis as it rose upwards alongside his belly. As the silent minutes passed he became overcome with the familiar overwhelming sense of pleasure that took control of his body, the images of naked women flashing across his mind, including the young lady from some rich family that had spread her legs for him the night before. Soon the pleasure grew too much for him to control, and in a short yet desperate moment he climaxed into a heady orgasm.

"Aaaaah fuck that was awesome!"

Relieved, he cleaned up just enough so that his maid, Maria, wouldn't notice anything, and then stepped into the shower, stretching back under the jets of warm water that ran in rivulets down his smooth body. Content, Eduardo drifted into thought, reflecting on a scheme that had taken over a year to unfold, a brilliantly masterminded plan.

"Darling is that you? Okay I'll buzz you through."

Eduardo drove up the cobbled drive to his mother's splendid *Gavéa* mansion with its spectacular view over *Leblon* and *Ipanéma*. The mansion had been built some sixty years earlier and was principally of brick and plaster construction with large shuttered windows and a magnificent terraced garden with cropped grass, flowerbeds, and water fountains. There were two gardeners working the bed of orchids off to the side of the driveway and they paused briefly to look up at Eduardo as he rolled by in his magenta Porsche.

He parked the car beside the house, taking a moment to adjust his shorts and look about. The garden surrounding the mansion was perfect, a quiet oasis in the madness of Rio de Janeiro. The only sounds were those of the birds in the trees and the creaking of cicadas in the branches above. The air was heavy, sign of an impending tropical storm – the summer monsoons that washed the city clean of her sins.

He walked to the front of the house, waiting for Maria, the house servant to open the door. "Master Eduardo, *que prazer*!"

"*Oi* Maria. Where is mama?"

"At the back. Go through the house, it's easier."

He walked past the maid, strolling confidently down the hallway into the large tiled living room that spilled down several stairs to a wide sunroom, enclosed with a series of French patio doors. The room was luxurious – his mother had spent a fortune making it what she claimed to be the most magnificent piece of decorating in Rio de Janeiro.

He pushed open the French patio doors, stepping out into the brilliant sunshine and onto the tiled exterior that ran alongside the Olympic-sized swimming pool. His mother was on the lawn on the far side of the pool. She was dressed in her white silk gown and holding a drink in her hand, her magnificent mane of auburn hair running over her shoulders and down her long slender back.

"How are you my dear?" She asked, her brilliant green eyes smiling, as she leaned forward to kiss Eduardo on the cheek.

"Very good mother. Excellent news today, I would never have imagined that things would have worked out so perfectly."

"What did father say when you spoke to him earlier?" He asked.

"He was cold as usual. You know how much he hates talking to me - the miserable bastard. But he was definitely saddened."

"I hope he'll fall into a depression and blame himself for the whole affair if you ask me. After all, it was he who decided to fire Carlos Varas. " She said.

They walked alongside the pool, taking in the magnificent sunny view below. Eduardo looked at his mother. Margaret was a remarkable woman who knew how to pick her battles. When her husband had decided to side with Eduardo's brother she had taken a stand, blaming him for David's gayness and Eduardo's drug problems, saying he had been a poor father, a man that had been too preoccupied with his business dealings to be around for the children.

Yet Eduardo secretly knew she was as much a culprit as his father. Her frequent parties and constant parade of young male lovers, many of them Eduardo's friends, was nothing short of scandalous - a constant source of embarrassment for both Eduardo and his brother. Nonetheless, his mother's frivolous behaviour paled in comparison to the menace his brother had presented. Not only had David's close relationship to their father been a threat to both Eduardo and his mother's inheritance, his brother's homosexuality had also been tremendously embarrassing for them both.

When the timing was right, Eduardo and Margaret had shown no hesitation in seizing the opportunity to cleanly eliminate David De Silva. In fact it had been Eduardo's mother who had decided to use Faustino and the Varas family as the catalysts to have David killed. She had learnt of Faustino's jealous passion for Chico, Isabella Varas' lover, and how in jealousy he double-crossed the drug lord and had him assassinated by the police. Margaret had also masterminded Julia Varas' kidnapping and the subsequent arrangement to have Faustino neatly eliminated by Carlos Varas.

"Do you believe father will pass more of his estate to us?" Asked Eduardo.

"Darling, how could he not! I already told you I went to the lawyers to get us more money following David's death. Imagine if he turned it down! I can just see how that would go in the press: 'Mr. De Silva denies distraught wife and surviving son additional financial support after death of sibling.'…"

"…Come on dear, let's get another drink shall we." She muttered.

"Antonio, please prepare lunch will you. We are awfully hungry, and I don't have much time since the ladies are expecting me for cards tonight!"

"Yes Ms. De Silva", mumbled the servant as he passed Eduardo his favourite drink, a vodka lemon on ice.

"Cards tonight? Where are you off to?" He asked.

"Ah to Marie's. You know the French crowd. We are having a French evening with a bit of gambling...nothing too serious though."

"Mama, I thought you said the gambling was done."

"Eduardo dear, with daddy's new funding we have plenty of cash to satisfy our needs, enough even for you to prop up another slum lord to replace the newest dead one...besides, the mayor's wife is expected to be there, so I'll be able to have a word with her regarding the next state election campaign and your role in it."

"Ah mother, you never stop do you!" winked Eduardo.

"Nothing gets in my way my darling, especially when it concerns the future of my son. Even if it means that I have to spend the evening with the most unsavoury and boring collection of human beings imaginable..."

"You wouldn't care to join your poor mother for the affair?" She joked.

"Sorry mama, I do believe my abilities would best be put to practice elsewhere." he smiled.

Margaret

The dinner party was a bore as usual. Margaret De Silva detested her French crowd, much preferring her more upbeat collection of British contemporaries who were more anchored in reality. It was most annoying how the rather overly-flamboyant collection of expatriate Parisians constantly moaned about how miserable life was in the third world. At times she simply wanted to turn around and slap some of them, reminding them that if it were not for Brazil and its endless riches and magnificent climate, they would probably still be in some dreary suburban *l'Île de France* neighbourhood cursing the grey skies and constant rain. However, Margaret had come to this party for one specific objective: to speak to the mayor's wife regarding the upcoming elections. So as pathetic as the company was she put on a pleasant face and worked the room to the best of her abilities.

Ah yes, the mayor's flimsy wife. Personally she detested the woman, finding her to be somewhat of a cackling fool who was short on everything, especially money. Ms Margaret De Silva knew that lady was none other than a fund collector for her pathetic crook of a husband, and that her presence at these card games was a convenient way for her to tap into the rich and powerful spouses of Rio's elite. Margaret was one of those, who despite her divorce form the city's richest man still had plenty of money and influence to ensure things went her way.

Margaret was independently wealthy of her husband, having been born into a powerful Brazilian family that had arrived in the country back in the time of early Portuguese settlement. In fact, history records her forefathers as having had a significant role in the Imperial Court that ruled Brazil's far-flung empire during the eighteenth and nineteenth centuries.

She was an only child, who had grown up under a lavish lifestyle supported by parents who knew how to wield political influence. They had ensured her match with Luis De Silva, taking much care to place their beautiful daughter in a social circle that would permit as much access as possible to the city's rising elite.

Margaret remembered her first encounter with Luis, who at the time was a shy yet determined son of a billionaire, deeply involved in his studies in journalism at the country's leading university – *Universidade Federal do Rio de Janeiro*. He was also preparing his academic career for an imminent departure to the United States to complete a Ph. D, and work for one of his father's subsidiaries in New York.

The two had fallen for each other quickly; Margaret seduced by the young man's stunning charm, and Luis by the young lady's beauty. They were married by the end of Luis' university program, and then off to the United States, where she spent three years studying Liberal Arts at Columbia University while her husband worked the New York real estate scene within his father's emerging American business.

Margaret quickly adopted the role of a supportive wife, attending every social activity and participating in every initial business decision that her husband made in those early New York days. She was present every night, directing the maids in the kitchen as they prepared dinner for the couple's growing New York social circle, an ensemble that included some of the most significant names in finance, banking, and real estate.

Their first child, David was born in New York while she was still at school. He was a beautiful baby, who despite his early shyness never ceased to turn the heads of jealous mothers when the couple strolled through Central Park on Sunday afternoons. The decision to have David had been an easy one; however, the decision to have him in America had been a challenge. Initially Luis fought with his wife, insisting the two return to the familiarity of Brazil for childbirth. Luis was concerned about the eroding political situation under Nixon, as well as the possibility that the Vietnam War could mean the end of America as a world power. Yet Margaret stood her ground against her husband, claiming there was nothing to lose in giving their first son a second passport.

As she saw it, and her husband had to agree, there was simply too much economic mass in the United States for the country to ever go down from a war in some distant land. The two both agreed that Vietnam would probably end in an American withdrawal – as it did a year after David's birth – and that the country would simply move on and find new purpose.

Margaret liked to remind her ex-husband how it had been she who had given David the papers to go live in America - something he liked to deny. To her it was just a misfortune that the privilege of being American had been bestowed on her first son and not on her second.

She had always been more attached to Eduardo, greatly preferring her younger son's more visible demonstration of masculinity as opposed to David's shyness. As a strong woman married to a formidable husband it frustrated her that her younger son was so athletically driven, while her older child preferred the obscure world of books, music, and art, something she considered to be the domain of girls.

David had always preferred his books and music to sports and socializing, signs of a future gayness that she had chosen to ignore. It had frustrated her to no end that her first child lacked the strength of her second boy, and it was there that the wedge between she and her husband grew, as Luis supported his older son's talent for music and academics, sending him to private schools and encouraging their academically gifted son with the best of tutors possible. Margaret truly believed it a misfortune that she had not been able to treat her oldest son's abnormality early on in life. Unlike her husband, she remained certain that if she could have intervened early enough with David, and corrected his aversion to masculine endeavours, he would never have become gay.

Yet while David played piano and tripped all over the place on the football pitch, Eduardo proved to be a phenomenal athlete, winning trophies at every athletic competition he entered. At school his progress was definitely more ordinary than David's; however, his physical stature and athletic skill captured his mother's eye, and she soon picked him as her favourite amongst the two boys.

She was drawn by her younger son's masculinity, convinced that if she groomed him right he would someday rise to positions of substantial power and influence in Rio de Janeiro. Those positions included a role in politics, essential to enabling both he and Margaret to someday surpass the level of power and wealth that her husband wielded.

It was for this reason Margaret had taken to courting the annoyingly boring ladies of the political elite, seeing them as the gatekeepers to her final objective: Eduardo as Governor of the State of Rio de Janeiro.

"Alicia, how are you tonight darling?" Margaret cried.

"Ah Margaret, so good to see you! So long since we last saw each other! I am delighted you were able to make it tonight, we have an absolutely marvellous group on hand for cards, a truly wonderful gathering of ladies!" Chirped the woman.

"Thrilling dear, I am dying to play cards. How long it has been since I had a good evening, especially since all of the horrors that have befallen the family over the past year…"

"Ah yes, my condolences to both you and Luis regarding David. We haven't seen each other much since it happened."

"Tell me how are Luis and Eduardo doing?" Alicia asked, a look of sympathy drifting across her face.

"Well Luis took things very hard, he has completely immersed himself in his work, and you know the thing with his former driver today…just horrid, horrid…Eduardo has begun to come around quite a bit since his brother's death. I think he was terribly depressed following the divorce, and certainly his brother's death did nothing to help. I hope he will be able to pull through, since he so much promise."

"Speaking of which Alicia, Eduardo was wondering if he would be able to meet with your husband. He is quite interested in the upcoming state election for Rio de Janeiro and wanted to know how he could become involved at a political level…you know it's about that age that our young men start thinking about these sorts of things. He so desperately wants to make a difference…do something for the community, in particular in the area of violence and crime, which of course have directly affected us so much as a family."

Alicia's face lit up with enthusiasm. "Yes the woman really is as idiotic as she looks", was all that Margaret could think.

"Certainly Margaret! I will pass that on to Ricardo tomorrow when he returns from the trade meeting in Brasilia. I am sure he would be thrilled to meet with Eduardo."

The objective of the evening had been achieved, and for the rest of the night Margaret spent her time wasting money on lavish card games and making small talk with the old girls about all sorts of things. Yet the main topic of the evening was of course the dreadful church shooting in *Ipanéma* that morning.

All of the ladies were terribly shocked that something of the sort could happen in the middle of the day in their neighbourhood.

As one of the women put it, "For heaven's sake does that mean we have to start putting metal detectors at the entrances to churches…I always thought it was only the poor Jews that had to deal with those sorts of things. I mean my Jewish friends, the pour souls, they constantly have to deal with those things when the go to services."

Everyone was most sympathetic to Margaret, realizing that it had been her driver that had caused all the fracas, yet most of them sympathized with the poor man, and several ladies said they would have done the same thing if they had of known who had kidnapped and murdered their daughter. One of the ladies went further saying, "God the man must have been distraught after all those things, losing his job, and his wife becoming some sort of deranged murderer killing innocent people. Tragic, so tragic."

"Worse that it was your poor sweet David who lost his life…Margaret." Said one of the ladies at the card table.

Margaret nodded, and used the discussion as a convenient excuse to retire, saying that the events of the day and the memory of her late son were too much to bear for the moment.

Everyone was most understanding, each taking a break from their game of cards to give Margaret an embrace and a gentle smile, while Alicia drifted from the room to have her butler call up Margaret's driver to take Ms. De Silva home.

"Ghastly, the poor woman, I don't know how she copes…"mumbled one of the ladies once Margaret was gone.

"Yes, terrible, terrible…life just is not fair at all."

Chapter VI

Luis - New York eighteen months later

Luis De Silva had never imagined such misery could befall a man in so short a time. It seemed just yesterday that he had divorced his wife to set a new path for his son David and himself. Yet how suddenly life can change: in a moment his son had been taken from him, his life turned upside down. Two and half years had passed since those tragic moments, when David's life was cut short just at a moment when he was entering the summer of his life, about to embark on adventures in the United Stated with a loving life partner, João.

Why, why David, and why at that moment in time? Was it not supposed to be that sons buried their fathers, and not the other way around?

And João, how tragic it had been to see his son-in-law, the day before a magnificent young man with so much promise, reduced to nothing, a broken boy lying in a hospital bed, his spirit wrenching in the agony of his loss.

The day of the murder was the last time that Luis saw João - since that moment in the hospital he had been unable to muster the courage to find out what had become of him in the months following the tragedy. Too embroiled in the shock of his own loss, he could not even contemplate the thought of re-establishing contact with either João or his family, even though a day never passed without him thinking about the boy. How was he? Where was he? Had he found someone else, or was he still sick?

"Sometimes the past is best left alone."

In the months that had followed his son's death Luis passed his business dealings off to his assistants as he attempted to come to terms with the changes he needed to face. He spent time wandering the globe, leaving Rio de Janeiro to spend time in France, before coming back to Brazil to cloister himself in his beachfront apartment.

Without his attention his businesses languished, as his assistants found themselves without direction, like a ship without a captain at the helm. Realizing he could lose everything, including a business that had been the culminating effort of both him and his father, Luis decided to pull himself together immersing himself in his only remaining passion, his work.

With new purpose, Luis De Silva returned to the working world more ruthless than ever, surprising long-time rivals who had expected him to have lost both his drive and passion. His businesses grew faster than ever before as he began shifting more and more of his activities outside of Brazil and into more promising emerging markets in Eastern Europe and Asia.

As the months passed he spent more time overseas, building his new head offices in New York City, where he was better equipped to handle problems hands-on as opposed to constantly struggling with the immense distances that came with living in a city as isolated from the rest of the world as Rio de Janeiro. He began calling New York his home, letting Rio de Janeiro and the past go.

It was on the second anniversary of his son's death that Luis De Silva finally realized at a subconscious level that he had begun to start dealing with the loss of his son. By passing more time in New York as opposed to Brazil he had in fact escaped from a world he really no longer wished to be a part of – a world of insecurity, oppression, class structures, and corruption.

How ironic it was that it was he and not his son who had escaped to New York. At times Luis felt as though he was living his son's dream, as if his boy's spirit had come to settle in his heart, directing Luis away from a world that had, unaware to him, begun to strangle his own spiritual existence.

Manhattan: a million different cultures living in pulsating harmony, a centre of creativity and vitality where sheer determination wins respect and success, giving hope to those without money, but with the brawn and the ideas to make it happen. Yes so much in contrast to the maddening corruption and self-beautification of Rio de Janeiro, where the vibrancy of the middle and lower classes are kept at bay, protecting the rich.

In New York one could find anything the heart desired, without the fear of violent crime and social decay that was so omnipresent in Brazil.

"Ahhh New York, I love you!" he thought as he walked silently down along West 72nd towards Central Park, after having one of the most magnificent dinners he had ever had.

A full stomach and the warmth of the early summer evening air sent his mind wandering, once again back to the past, as he reflected on the two and a half years since David's death. How odd it was that his son's murder never had been completely solved. The police had attributed it to Isabella Vara's affair with the *favela* drug baron by the name of Chico, an affair that had led to the poor woman finding herself caught up in a game beyond her imagination, an affair that took her family down, ending with Carlos Varas' suicide eighteen months ago.

"It had been eighteen months!" he though to himself, my God, it seems just like yesterday that he had received a call from the police informing him of his former driver's murder-suicide in an *Ipanéma* church just after Christmas, and only a couple of weeks prior to the first anniversary of David's death.

Luis had been initially shocked by the brutality of the suicide, with an inkling of a sense of responsibility for the fortunes of the fallen man; however, any pity had been wiped away with the memories of his late son, and of Carlos' deranged wife. How had he ever considered hiring such a man, helping such a family? A man who had a track record as a common criminal during his youth and who had married a wife who committed adultery with one of Rio de Janeiro's most wanted drug criminals.

To this day he still did not understand why Isabella Varas had chosen violence to escape the trap she had put herself in. Rather than turn to reputable sources she elected to follow the kidnappers' demands, taking things into her own hands to try to save herself and her kidnapped daughter. Yet violence solves nothing, and in the end her actions, the destruction of a young and promising life, saved neither herself nor her daughter.

Luis tried to imagine the horror of the poor woman's final days of freedom – the knowledge that her daughter had been kidnapped, and the finality of the task to save her daughter and keep her affair secret from Carlos. In some ways he could understand how the circumstances left her with few options other than to undertake the murderous plot that would ultimately change the course of life for so many.

The Varas family had been a project for Luis, the occasion to take a young lower-middle class family, and give them opportunities rarely afforded to people of their class and stature in Brazil. They had been brought together by one of Luis' late military friends who had insisted he take on a knowledgeable and responsible military driver, "with the ending of military influence in the direction of the country, the place will only become more dangerous to those with power…" had insisted his friend.

Luis had liked Carlos. He was reliable with a strict work ethic founded on deep religious values, a stringent military career, and a difficult childhood. However, with the passing of the years, Luis suspected his driver's obsession for perfection went beyond his profession and into his family life, suffocating his wife and children. That obsession was more than likely the reason for his family's collapse – "excessive moral values are like a prison for those who have no say in the rules". Carlos had been a good man; sadly he had been a captive of his own past, born into a country rife with social decay.

In the years prior to David's death, Luis had held an unbending belief that the social decay in the country could best be dealt with by building on the political institutions of the country. Sure there were small differences that one could make, as Luis had done with the Varas family; however, by providing funds and direction to the nation's political class one could ensure change on a broader scale. Luis' attitude was that the mess was best left to the politicians who had the time and the skills to deal with the country's massive socio-economic problems.

As a result, through his numerous business ventures, he funnelled millions of dollars to political parties promising to do the things on his wish list, taking a *laissez-faire* attitude, and stepping in only when things got out of hand on trade issues, excessive business taxes, or rising crime.

With his son's passing he realized in many ways he and his business friends were to blame for the mess in the country. If they had taken a more active role in dealing with delinquency in the country's political circles many of the social problems that led to the collapse of families such as Carlos' would have been prevented. Perhaps that fateful day, now nearly two and a half years ago, would never have happened. Perhaps destiny would have been different, and today and it would have been David and João walking together on Central Park, rather than a lonely old man without a son.

Yet the past was the past, and Luis was not one to spend his life living in the shadows of something he could never change. In New York he rediscovered his spirit and in doing so began to shift his life over to the United States, eventually buying himself a new apartment just near 5th Avenue and East 63rd Street, a quick limousine ride from his work down in the financial district. With the passage of time he also met a new lady friend, nothing physical, but someone to fill a void from the many losses over the past few years.

From Brazil his ex-wife continued to harass him for money, this time saying Eduardo needed funding for his imminent political launch in state elections scheduled for the middle of next year. Luis did not really care too much, he remained convinced his second son was nothing short of a common criminal, whose drug problems and suspicious friendships were symptomatic of a profound mental problem. Luis wondered about Eduardo. Had it been his fault that the young man had turned out the way he was, or was it the fact that Margaret had gotten to the boy first?

Eduardo had always been Margaret's, and David his. That's the way things had always been, and that's the way they always would be. If she believed the boy had future in politics it was his duty to send her the money so that she could open the doors for him, whether or not he agreed.

Standing on the balcony of his sophisticated Manhattan apartment, he looked out on a world so different from the one he had known two and half years ago, the day before his son had died. The sky was a crimson red as the sun dipped down over Central Park. Traffic streamed by on the crowded streets below, as hundreds of pedestrians scurried about at the end of the first of many glorious summer days to come.

Luis turned his back to the scene below. It was time to turn in, he was exhausted and didn't want to be in bed too late since in the morning he had another meeting followed by a lunchtime fitness session with his personal trainer at the club. There was also dinner with his new girlfriend, and he knew he would need to be in top form for that.

So after a refreshing shower he turned in, sliding under the comfort of his crisp sheets, newly pressed by his New York house servant, a quiet Filipino by the name of Maria. His book was placed on the bedside table, along with a small bowl of mint chocolates, a bedtime delight he taken to over the past few years.

"Good-morning-Luis-time-to-wake-up! The-time-is-six-thirty-A-M-and-the-weather is-sunny-and-eighty-two-degrees-with-seventy-five-per-cent-relative-humidity..."

Luis rolled over in bed, rubbing his eyes while the synthetic voice of his alarm clock switched from New York weather to Bach organ and church music.

He stretched, turned off the radio, and rolled over for the television remote, flicking the channels to CNN Financials to pick up the early morning news as well as the latest opinions on interest rates and the currency markets. Awake, he swung out of bed, walking past his workout gear laid out in the bathroom, Maria having placed it there the day before in anticipation of his hectic morning schedule.

Luis always wore his fitness clothes to work, preferring to shower at the office after a brisk morning walk and change into his suits there. The whole procedure was so much less complicated, especially during the excessively clammy summers and frigid winters that this city was all too well known for. As far as he was concerned there was nothing worse than arriving at the office in a soggy suit.

Dressed and freshened up, he padded through the living room to the front door, picking up the morning paper and some post that had been deposited outside his door by the doorman.

The newspaper was small, not unusual for a weekday; however, what was unusual was the small pink envelope standing out from the customary collection of bills and accounts. It was addressed to him, in vaguely familiar handwriting that immediately caught his attention.

Luis walked over to the lounge window, absorbing the activity below as Central Park gradually brightened under the early morning sun. The morning bustle of another rush hour was just beginning – New York on a weekday.

He peeled open the envelope, extracting a single sheet of plain white paper addressed to him. Luis paused, staring at the letter in his hands.

> *Mr. De Silva this is João, your late son David's ex-boyfriend.*
>
> *I know it has been sometime since we last saw each other and many things have since passed under the bridge, yet I feel it is important that we meet again. I am in New York, having finally accepted the offer at Columbia to lecture here…a long story.*
>
> *I need you to let me know if we can meet tonight for dinner at the Baker's Street Café in the SOHO at 8PM. You can confirm by leaving a message on my cell phone at 999-555-1234. I await your response.*
>
> *Fond wishes,*
>
> *João N.*

Luis was stunned; surprised to receive a message from someone he believed he would never see again. Taken off guard, he stood there contemplating his next move, uncertain as to whether or not meeting the young man was the best thing to do. Perhaps it was better to leave him and his boy in the past.

Yet his heart felt otherwise - João had contacted him for a reason, and he owed it to this boy and to his David to sit down once and for all and deal with the terrible anguish of the past. Listening to his heart, Luis picked up the phone, waiting as the call was forwarded to a voice mail. The greeting message was João's voice, so soft and sweet, a gentle reminder in English and in Portuguese of the tender young man who had once been so a part of Luis' world.

After leaving a confirmation message, Luis left another on his girlfriend's phone, apologizing that he would need to cancel their date for the night because of an urgent family issue. Then, looking at his watch, he realized the lateness of the hour and dashed out the front door, making double time on the street so as not to cut too much into his preparation time at the office.

João

João gazed silently from the window of his bedroom apartment in SOHO, watching the early morning sun as it drifted steadily skywards above an awakening Manhattan skyline.

He had been in New York just a year, recent enough that he never seemed to tire of the city's incredible skyline, its endless diversity, its inconceivable freedom of movement and security. New York was a blur of energy, speed, and creativity: twenty million people coming and going in a never-ending rush towards hopes, dreams, and aspirations. Here on this tiny island no more than a few blocks wide, in this epicentre of the human race, dreams became reality.

He remembered his first days in the city the year before – rushing about on whirlwind tours of Brooklyn, the SOHO, the Eastside, the Bronx, Jersey, Staten Island, and the Statue of Liberty, in taxis and ferries. New York was so massive and incredibly accessible - João knew Sao Paulo well; however, not even *Sampa* could compare with what was here. New York City knew no limits because there really were none. Unlike Sao Paulo, there were no vast slums ringing the city and closing it in under a stifling stranglehold of violent crime. New York was alive, surging with vivacity – the very centre of the world.

Coming to New York City was key to João's recovery. By escaping from Rio de Janeiro, he knew he would be able to put a painful past behind him as he sought desperately to forget his anguish. It had been two and a half years since his David had been taken away from him - the memories of the days and months following his death forever etched in his brain.

He remembered how he had cried in the arms of his mother as he tried to come to terms with the fact that the man he loved had been taken away from him in one brutal moment. It had been too much to bear: the pain of being alone, the inevitable devastating return to an empty apartment that had once been home to such love and happiness. Then the return to hospital, the visits with therapists, the medications, the unanswered letters to David's father, the visit to David's tombstone, and finally a failed attempt at suicide.

Pain, so much pain.

Over the months following his attempted suicide, João's life slowly began to piece itself together under the watchful eyes of his friends and family, his emotions passing from grief, to hate, to sadness, to rage, and finally to forgiveness. João found forgiveness because of all of the emotions he was forced to endure, it was the only one that seemed to offer any hope of peace.

Peace for himself and for David.

Armed with forgiveness, he decided to meet the woman who had taken David from him. In talking to her face to face, he hoped to find answers, answers to the dark secrets lurking behind David's death, a death shrouded in mystery behind the silent insanity of a murderer gone mad.

Three days before he was scheduled to meet Isabella Varas in person at the state penitentiary, she was found dead, strung up in a noose of bed sheets in her prison cell. Her suicide thwarted João's attempt at finding closure. It prevented him from finding answers, from learning why a woman from such an ordinary and middle-class background would in the space of so short a time commit acts of such horror and incomprehension.

There was foul play, of that João was certain. There were simply too many coincidences behind the death of David: suicide, kidnapping, murder, and a bizarre proximity in the relationship between the Varas and De Silva families.

João began his quest to learn more about Isabella, the Varas family, and their tie to his late partner's family. Through court documents, he was able to discover Isabella's affair with a man named Chico, a powerful drug lord in the city's slums, who prior to David's murder was gunned down by the police following a tip from an anonymous source. According to official circles the source was never identified and the relationship between Isabella and Chico was nothing more than a brief affair between two complete strangers. Yet João doubted the explanation, believing there was more than the police knew or wished him to know.

Determined to find answers, in the weeks that followed he used bribes and family influence to obtain information from the police, discovering how money could uncover even the best of best kept secrets. He learnt that the tip that led to Chico's death had come from within Chico's inner circle, of which the most likely suspect was that of a rising star by the name of Faustino.

Faustino was the leading suspect because of his unusually close relationship to Chico. Police records showed that both Faustino and Chico, in addition to having been seen together hundreds of times in public, had on numerous occasions rented hotel rooms for single night stays in various locations in the *Lapa* area over the course of several years. Furthermore, records showed testimonies from witnesses implicating the two of them in the murder of two armed men, after a brutal struggle in a *Lapa* hotel room several years earlier.

The discovery was of no surprise to João. He had always been convinced that homosexual practice was widespread in Brazilian society, even amongst poorer or lesser-educated social circles. It was just that in these parts of society gayness was not expressed as gayness, rather it was undefined, kept more within the realms of sexual need, as opposed to full emotional attachment.

To confirm his discovery, he hired two former Federal Police officers to monitor Faustino and his activities. Through his agents, João discovered that following Chico's death Faustino had disappeared from drug trafficking, almost dropping out of the drug world, before returning with a vengeance to rapidly establish his control of drugs in Rio de Janeiro's largest slum - *Rocinha*. His reappearance had literally reshaped the slums, bringing a gun-enforced end to weeks of bloody fighting amongst kingmakers for Chico's old territory.

As he followed Faustino and the Varas family, João also had his men quietly investigate the De Silva family, in the hope that he would be able to establish a link between Faustino, Chico, Isabella Varas, and the De Silva clan. He began with Eduardo – an individual that at the best of times he cordially disliked.

João and Eduardo hated each other from the moment they had met - João's intellectual and artistic social circles clashed with Eduardo's more macho world of kickboxing and gyms. At gatherings of the children of Rio's social elite – about the only time the two crowds met - Eduardo never hesitated to pass the odd drunken veiled threat. João hardly feared the boy; however, he knew David had an unspoken fear of his aggressive sibling, at times mentioning he was sure Eduardo wanted nothing less than have him out of the way so he could get more money from papa.

João knew Eduardo hated him and David for the close relationship they shared with his father. Eduardo also made it clear he blamed David for the collapse of their parent's marriage and the subsequent "hardship" his mother had endured. Of course everyone knew Ms. De Silva was far from hard times, having access to well-provisioned bank accounts and a mansion in *Gavéa* that rivalled those in the hills of Monaco.

João began to have Eduardo followed. He had his police team tap all the phones the young man had, and slowly over time he learned the extent of the young man's involvement in drugs, both as a buyer and as a dealer. As the picture grew clearer, it became evident that Eduardo had also been discretely providing weapons to Chico and Faustino's clan over the past couple of years, in exchange for access to drugs and possibly other favours.

The discovery was staggering, and João was tempted to go public and have Eduardo exposed in the courts; however, he knew he still lacked direct proof, and it was highly improbable he would ever be able to get a man like Faustino onto a witness stand alive, to testify against someone as powerful as Eduardo De Silva.

Then as if his thoughts were being read, Faustino was executed in an Ipanéma church just after Christmas. The drug boss was apparently attending weekday services, something he had been doing since the days of his youth as an abandoned child at an Evangelical missionary school in the *favela*. His murderer, who then turned the gun on himself, was Carlos Varas - the husband of the woman who had killed David just a year before.

João knew something was afoot, that someone powerful had manipulated Faustino and Carlos Varas, eliminating them so as to forever erase any path to David's real killers. João was convinced that powerful individual was Eduardo, and perhaps even Eduardo's mother, Margaret.

.

Over the months that followed, João mercilessly tracked both Eduardo and Margaret De Silva, wanting to leave no stones unturned. He looked back into their past, collecting further evidence of Eduardo's drug links, his cocaine dependency, his mother's relationship with the political establishment, and their increased association with the drug ring once run by Chico and then by Faustino.

The scale of deceit, lies, corruption, manipulation, and murder was beyond imagination.

His well paid police operatives searched confidential police documents retrieved from Carlos Varas' *Copacabana* flat, finding notes and threats that had been sent to the Varas family from unnamed sources, as well a letter and a photo of Faustino that had been delivered by mail to Carlos Varas the day before he had murdered the drug lord. The letter clearly outlined the relationship between Isabella Varas and Chico, and the bitter love triangle involving a jealously isolated Faustino. It described in detail how Faustino had used a police tip to ambush and kill Chico, and how he had blackmailed an innocent Isabella into murdering David, using the Varas' kidnapped daughter as the prize.

The letter confirmed the relationship between the Varas family, and Chico and Faustino. More importantly though, it clearly established the motives behind David's murder, Isabella's suicide, and Carlos Varas' suicide killing of Faustino several months earlier. Yet it failed to prove an irrefutable link between Eduardo De Silva and the deceased drug lords.

João knew that if he could find that elusive link, possibly proving it had been Eduardo or his mother who had written the letters, he would have the evidence to put them in court for multiple homicide, extortion, blackmail, and corruption. There was no doubt in his mind that Eduardo and his mother were implicated - the motives were all there: removing David meant more inheritance funds, in turn affording greater power in what had become their apparent role in drugs, politics, and weapons.

He became obsessed with finding a link, spending the following months monitoring phone calls between Eduardo and Margaret De Silva, hoping that something would show up. He pushed his agents harder; taking risks that put both him and his investigators at jeopardy of being discovered. Yet despite all of his financial resources and determination, everything remained sealed tight - no leaks, and no leads. Frustrated, João found himself after so many months of work stonewalled - without any proof.

Discouraged, exhausted, and realizing his investigation could begin to put him in harm's way, he decided it would be prudent to put his efforts aside for some time. The moment was opportune, since for the past year Columbia University had been waiting patiently for him to accept an offer of employment as a professor, a position he had passed on during the difficult months following David's death.

The university's department of economics had begun to up their ante, making it clear that they wanted João's academic ability in time for a series of courses and research projects that had been on hold for the past year and a half while he dealt with David's loss.

After much reflection, as well as insistence from concerned family and friends who believed his obsessive investigation into David's death was of no good for his mental health, João decided to go to New York. He figured that a semester abroad presented the perfect opportunity for him to find some peace in a new environment with different people. Besides he thought, "Perhaps the time away would open new avenues to Eduardo and Margaret role in David's murder."

Sixteen hours after a teary goodbye to family and friends at Rio de Janeiro's *Antonio Carlos Jobim* International Airport, João exited United States Customs and Immigration to the warm welcome of two university professors from Columbia's department of economics. João already knew both men fairly well, having met them in person during the interview process over a year and a half ago, when he and David had come up from Brazil to investigate opportunities in New York.

The taller of the two professors, Dr. Jacob Stephens, was a bit older than João. He was handsome and athletic, with well-groomed receding hair, green eyes, and a lighter complexion. He was a pleasant individual, with a contagious beaming grin, which had even João smiling for the first time in months.

The other man, Dr. Anderson, was the new departmental chairman. He was a shorter more heavy-set bespectacled man with an English accent, and unlike Dr. Stephens, he had a thick mop of curly dishevelled grey hair. João recalled Dr. Anderson having a large family and that they lived in the Brooklyn Heights area in a magnificent Brown Stone home near the water. He and David had been invited to a department dinner at the man's house during their last New York trip together.

"João, how are you? Are you doing better, so much bad news…" asked Jacob.

"I am…much better, you know time helps." He replied in his impeccable, yet lightly accented English.

"Good, we have all been thinking of you here in New York." Pausing, he continued, "Just to refresh your memory, this is

Dr. Keith Anderson, our new departmental chair, though I am sure you remember him well."

"Yes I do, yes I do! We had dinner at your house in Brooklyn!" declared João.

Anderson smiled warmly, reaching out to shake João's hand, before exclaiming in his jovial British accent, "Come on then, let's get out of this bloody airport and get this young man to your apartment Jacob!"

They continued their conversation on the way out to the parking lot. In a rather fatherly fashion, Keith Anderson took João's luggage buggy, insisting the younger man relax after such a long journey.

New York spilled out before him as they drove into the city from JFK. The gigantic skyscrapers, the masses of people, the bright lights, and the cacophony of well dressed people and expensive cars – so foreign, so different to Rio de Janeiro. It was thrilling. "My God it feels good to be here!" thought João.

Over the next week, which was eventually extended to two and then three, João fell in love with the city, staying with Jacob at his apartment in the SOHO. The older man's company was wonderful, providing much needed companionship. Everyday was an adventure as they toured New York inside out, from the Bronx to Columbia University, Chelsea to SOHO, and Times Square to Central Park. João knew Jacob was wooing him, doing his best to convince him to spend more than one semester in the "Big Apple".

Jacob, and indeed the entire economics department at Columbia, were convincing, and so was New York. Finally, on a gorgeous summer afternoon, João caved in, accepting Stephen's pleas over ice cream in Central Park.

"João, you'll love it! New York is just what you need to get away from Rio de Janeiro." He paused, before continuing slowly, "I know David is gone, but you cannot keep living your life in the past. Look at you, you are such a magnificent brilliant young man, with so much going for you. I am sure - no I correct myself - I am certain that David would have wanted you to be here, to live this dream."

João looked up at Jacob, staring at him in the eyes. There was a moment of silence, as the two men gazed at each other, feelings, electricity, and tenderness passing across the short distance that separated them.

Jacob smiled, "*Shalom mon ami*" he whispered.

João smiled back, "S*halom*."

João and Jacob spent the remaining days of July and early August falling passionately in love, wandered the city together, living the moment, as they soaked up the tolerance and diversity of Manhattan. By mid-August João's trip had turned into a three-week affair and his growing wardrobe of New York fashion had begun to fill Jacob's room. They were passionately in love, deciding that João would move in permanently starting in September, after a short two-week trip back to Rio de Janeiro to finalise visas and bring more personal items back with him.

João returned to Brazil to a surprise: there had been a breakthrough in his private investigation. Eduardo De Silva's house maid, Maria, had come discreetly forward to say that she had heard Mrs. De Silva and Eduardo plotting out murder and that she had found papers lying around in Eduardo's computer room - drafts of letters that had not been put through the shredder. She had stolen the letters, knowing they were valuable, and had offered to sell them to João's agents for a fair amount of money in cash.

João did not hesitate - he instructed his men to pay amply for the letters as well as provide enough cover and funds for Maria to quietly disappear into the safety of obscurity. He also decided to reward his two agents, providing them with comfortable bonuses for their good work.

Armed with copies of all the evidence, which he burned onto CD's, João knew he finally had a case to charge Margaret and Eduardo De Silva with the murders of Carlos, Isabella, and their daughter, as well as Faustino, and Chico; however, most importantly he knew, with the evidence in his hands, he could bring them down in the murder of David De Silva.

The breakthrough was breathtaking - how suddenly it had happened! After so much struggle and suffering over the past year and a half since David's death, he finally had closure. Yet with all the evidence in hand, and the investigation closed, João felt a sense emptiness. Those sheets of papers were the final moments plotted around David's existence, his David's existence. In a twisted way, the mystery behind David's death had somehow prolonged their relationship, and now that the murder was solved, it seemed as though David really was no more.

João was saddened, yet at the same time he realized his new love for Jacob, and that it was his duty to put David to rest, to finally allow both of them to find peace. "Arrhh!! Why do things have to be so complicated, so terribly complicated?" He thought to himself.

With all of this on his mind, he decided it was best for him to leave Brazil and reflect on the situation from the safety of New York, electing to return as soon as possible to Manhattan, to rejoin Jacob.

Back in New York, João settled quickly into Jacob's apartment, taking the remainder of the month of August to feel at home. The weather was hot, real hot, as hot as Rio de Janeiro in January, but without the easy access to sea and ocean that came with living in *Ipanéma* and *Leblon*. João thrived in it, joining Jacob for jogging in Central Park between breaks at Columbia, and entertaining groups of young black kids near the university with antics on his guitar – yes João had returned to guitar for the first time since David's death, relishing in his incredible ability to use music as a way to shape people's emotions.

He also started setting up his office at Columbia, taking time to shelve his books and prepare for the upcoming semester. Fortunately he only had one course to lecture in the autumn; a fourth year course related to Latin American Economics, in particular Argentina following the Peso Devaluation. The department chose him for the course given his expertise in the field; furthermore, the students in the class were strong potential graduate school candidates for his area of research.

Having time for himself over the autumn was a be blessing - there was much to read. Yes João was a brilliant scholar; however his year and a half hiatus from the world of research had left him temporarily disconnected from his milieu. He knew that a semester of light teaching would help him find the time to study more specific areas, which he could eventually develop into graduate thesis work for future students. There was no doubt in his mind his original Ph. D. research would play a directing role for his work, in fact his thesis had been the central reason that Columbia's economics department had hired him, apart from the fact that he was one of the brightest young minds in economics to have come out of Latin America in some time.

João had a fundamentally free-market leaning paradigm to his work in economics; however, he also believed the economy as a whole had a moral and essential obligation to ensure that all of humanity benefited from the fruits of economic growth and innovation. His doctoral thesis, an insight into the marginalization of vast amounts of Brazil's population was the basis of his thinking, and it was with that in mind that he constructed his upcoming semester of lecturing at Columbia.

Over the long term, he also planned to use his position at Columbia to develop policy directives to be used by stakeholders in emerging market economies to integrate the poor into the real economy. Having the poor participate and benefit from the real economy would increase government tax revenues, hence providing resources to improve amenities, services, schools, and neighbourhoods. With improved infrastructure, incomes and opportunities would continue to rise for the poor, eventually lifting them out of poverty, and into the realm of the real economy. João believed that ultimately, albeit many years into the future, such an effort would eliminate crime and poverty in the giant slums of the world's emerging market economies.

In the quiet remaining days before the summer ended, João took to walking New York on a daily basis with guitar in hand, taking the time to talk to people on the streets and in different neighbourhoods. The experience connected him with the people of the city. He was astounded with just how proud New Yorkers were of their home, something that went beyond the physical beauty of the place, something that was more profound, a deep connect to a city that relished with pride.

This was in sharp contrast to Rio de Janeiro. Granted in Rio *Cariocas* had a strong connection with their city; however, their connection was more superficial, rarely going beyond an affinity for the city's marvellous geography. Fact: Rio de Janeiro was an ugly city in a beautiful setting, with no community spirit. The reality was that the vast majority of the city's residents disliked their city, calling crime, pollution, and poverty the leading causes of their disaffection. This only reinforced João's belief that if Rio de Janeiro could emulate other great cities such as New York, Montreal, and Paris in creating a stronger sense of pride and association in their city, then she would find a way out of the mess she had been engulfed in since the city fell into a decline following the departure of the political middle class to Brasilia in the early 1960's.

The problem was of course Rio de Janeiro's corrupt political and elite classes. The rich bribed the politicians for short-term gain and then footed the bill to finance the most corrupt candidates, by providing the funds to buy the votes of the disaffected. These policies had been going on since democracy had existed in Brazil, while prior to the institutionalization of a democratic system, the country's mixture of limited democracy and dictatorships had done little to help the bridge the gap between rich and poor.

The thoughts of the injustices in the Latin America weighed prominently on his mind as he began his first semester of lecturing at Columbia University. His students took quickly to the beautiful soft-spoken young man who flew back and forth before them, enjoying how with his lightly accented English, he was able to passionately argue his points of view. He was quick on the mark, blending reality with complex mathematical theory, more than enough to gain the loyalty and respect of his small class of thirteen students. His ability was astounding, perhaps even more so for the fact that he was as young, or if not younger than most of the students in the room.

One afternoon, after the class had ended, João was cleaning the marker board and packing his notes into his familiar leather briefcase, when one of his students, a young woman by the name of Elizabeth, approached him. "Dr. Nito, sorry to bother you, but the class is planning to go for drinks at one of the student pubs off campus, and we were wondering if you would like to join us."

João smiled, "I'd be delighted, though please, I beg you, don't call me Dr. Nito. It's way too formal, João is just fine."

"Joooa…uhh..ooops, how on earth do you say that?" She stuttered, turning a crimson red.

João laughed, he was used to Americans not being able to pronounce his name, in fact with Jacob it had taken days to finally have him saying it right.

"João" he said, "just like jo-ow".

"Ahh cool, I think I can get it, though do be patient with me," as she started to laugh.

The board clear of notes, and his briefcase packed, Elizabeth and João joined the other students in the class to amble leisurely through Columbia's campus to a small Irish pub not too far from the lecture hall. The air was cooler, as the eastern summer faded, giving way to fall, as they called autumn here. The leaves were green on the conifers; however, the deciduous trees had lost their sheen and had begun to turn a more jaded colour, reflecting the time of the year.

The pub was small and cozy, and the group of them settled down to what eventually would become a regular event every week, except during exam time. They drank several glasses and the students quizzed him about his life in Brazil, which they found most exotic.

That first night out João held back on some points, preferring to be reticent, since he had learnt through experience that too much information too quickly can lead to others judging too soon. Thus to begin with he spoke neither of his gayness, nor of his background as the son of a wealthy banking family. He also avoided talking about the pains of the past, preferring to wait until he knew his audience better.

However, as the weeks passed, and their intimate pub nights became a ritual, João began to open up, sharing more with his students. He spoke of his loving relationship with Jacob Stephens, the eminent Jewish economist, as well as his background of privilege in Brazil and how he had turned to both economics and music to express his dissatisfaction with the gulf between rich and poor in his homeland.

Love

The fire burned softly, adding to the mid-December feel in the air. The apartment was decorated with Chanukah and Christmas decorations, duty to both Jacob and João's birthrights.

Joao sat silently thinking. It was two years since David had died, nearly twenty-four months since tragedy had changed the path of his life. How fast his life had changed, how sudden and miraculous his recovery. Perhaps it had been Jacob, or maybe it had been the work he had done to track down those who had killed his David. That work was still with him – the documents stored in his office in their apartment, ready to be used when the time was right to go public.

Tears welled in his eyes as he sat there, looking at Jacob curled up on the sofa in his fluffy gown marking graduate student final exam papers. Sensing something was wrong, Jacob looked over at his boyfriend.

"Joãozinho, what's wrong baby?"

"Arhh, it's David, the memories… it's two years since he died now…"

"Ah baby, I didn't know. No wonder you're feeling like this. Here, let me get you something."

Jacob put away his papers and went to the kitchen to prepare tea and some biscuits. After a few minutes he returned, taking his place beside his boyfriend.

"Talk baby. Tell me what's on your mind."

João looked at Jacob, staring into his deep green eyes, hypnotized by their beauty.

"I know how David died." He blurted out. "I know it all, everything, and I have all the evidence here, with me. I've known for months, in fact since I was last back in Rio in August, but I didn't know what to do with it…" his voice breaking with emotion.

"But today…in the news on the Internet…at the department I saw something that shocked me, something I cannot accept!" he cried.

Jacob sat listening, waiting for his partner to organize his thoughts.

João continued. "Eduardo, David's younger brother is running for a position as a state deputy in Rio de Janeiro in the elections later this coming year. He's become involved in politics and is part of a coalition that will most likely win. He is popular in the slums, because he is young and street smart, but also because he has the right connections in the right places."

He paused. "Eduardo murdered his brother, my David."

There was a silence in the room, the weight of João's words sinking into Jacob's brain. Then all of a sudden João erupted into tears, shaking and sobbing in Jacob's arms.

After a few minutes of crying João seemed to pull himself together. He pulled away from his partner, and for the first time since they had been together, he said to Jacob that he was going to sleep in the guest room and would prefer to be left alone.

Over the next few days they spoke little, João and Jacob passing by each other in silence in the house. Jacob grew frustrated, unsure what to do and how to breach the silence between them.

Christmas passed and João left New York, to spend New Year in Rio de Janeiro with his family. After two weeks he did not return, eventually asking Jacob in an email to arrange a substitute to run his courses while he was away.

Their SOHO apartment was silent, as Jacob grew sadly used to the solitude. The days passed, turning into weeks, and eventually January gave way to February. There were calls, usually short, with João sounding overworked from slogging away on party nomination campaigns in the prelude to the upcoming elections.

In their brief conversations João promised to return to New York, but just did not know when, as he said, "I have unfinished business here. I have to work hard to ensure our party puts a candidate forward that can stop Eduardo from winning."

After five weeks of frustration, Jacob decided he needed to find out what had become of his boyfriend. "Had he lost himself to Rio de Janeiro? Would he ever return?"

Calling the department, he told the chairman he needed to have his courses substituted indefinitely, that he had to take immediate leave for personal reasons and did not know when he would return. The chairman, Keith Anderson asked few questions, since his respect for Jacob went beyond their simple working relationship. "Okay Jacob, I understand, I'll ask one of your grad students to fill in for you."

With that Jacob booked himself on a flight for Rio the very next evening, taking the day to pack and organize himself for his departure. He knew not what would be waiting for him in Brazil, a land and a world far from what he knew, unlike places such as Europe and Asia, with which he was much more familiar.

Jacob had always considered himself an educated and well-travelled man. He had been brought up that way, as the fifth son of an enormous Conservative Jewish family from Brooklyn Heights. His father had been a prominent New York financial broker in his day, and the family had gone on many trips, including business holidays to London and Israel. His old man had always preached education, sending all of his children to the best schools and providing them with college funds. Jacob in the end had not needed any funding, since his own academic ability proved to be extraordinary, and he was accepted into Yale as a young scholar on a full scholarship. Before electing to attend he used the college fund provided to him by his father for a one-year trip around the world.

During that year he spent time in Europe, Africa, and Asia, crossing the Soviet Union from East to West and seeing things that the average Westerner could only imagine. He had been able to make the crossing because of his Canadian passport, which he held through his mother, who had been born in Montreal. His travels also took him to Israel, where he spent four months working on a kibbutz learning Hebrew and French with other youngsters. Living on a kibbutz in the Middle East was an eye opener, as he witnessed the perilous relationship between Arab and Israeli in the 1980's. His stay in Israel shaped his own views on the Zionism, views that ultimately were too liberal for his father and mother, and in fact in the years to come it was his attitude about Zionism and Israel, and not his gayness, which came to separate him from his family.

Yet despite all of his travels, Jacob had never visited Brazil, always believing the place to be too violent and corrupt. As he sat on the plane he could not suppress the sense of trepidation he felt regarding his imminent foray into a land he hardly knew, to find a man he so passionately loved.

He awoke after a bad night's sleep in the crowded economy section of American Airlines, to the odour of overcooked eggs and soggy waffles wafting out from the trolleys being pulled down the isles by grumpy flight attendants. After breakfast and some time to freshen up, the plane began its gentle descent into Rio de Janeiro, the lights blinking occasionally as the pilot prepared the aircraft for landing through a dense layer of fog that covered the region around the international airport.

After a smooth landing, they taxied into the gate, arriving a little more than ten minutes late.

Jacob was travelling light, so once he had cleared customs he was able to stride straight out into the main hall, ignoring the soliciting from errant taxi drivers as he made his way straight towards a fellow holding a sign with his name written on it.

"*Senhor* Stephens, yes?" The man asked.

"Yes that would be me."

"Eeehhh, good!" he gleamed. "Follow me sir, this way, I am your driver for the hotel shuttle."

They roared into the city, tearing onto a wide freeway that initially passed the airport, but eventually cut through a gigantic array of cluttered suburban slums that stretched into infinity along the grey cityscape. The freeway soon snaked its way into the city centre, becoming a two level elevated highway that was crowded in by shadowy brick and concrete urban structures.

Staring out at the scenery, Jacob was struck by the similarities Rio seemed to share with pretty much any other third world metropolis. For all he knew he could be in South Africa, especially Cape Town, given the odd shaped mountain tops that dotted the landscape.

They arrived in *Ipanéma* at his beachfront hotel, fighting their way through a sea of traffic. So many people, and so many different shapes, forms, colours, and sizes. The only thing they seemed to have in common was that they were all wearing the minimum amount of clothing possible - probably because of the heat, which already had Jacob covered in sweat through his New York clothes – this despite the air conditioning in the car.

"Why so many people? Is this normal?" He asked.

"*Carnaval* my friend! *Muita festa*, lots of party!"

"Carnival, I thought that was next week?"

"Yes sir, but the party starts before then!"

"Oh God", was all Jacob could think. If there was one thing he could not stand was the combination of crowds and tropical heat.

As soon as he was in his room he raced for the telephone, calling João's Rio de Janeiro telephone number, a number he rarely answered when Jacob called from New York.

The phone rang twice, and then João's familiar soft sensual voice picked up. He sounded tired, very tired.

"*Oi, quiem fala?*"

"Ahhh…João it's me." He gasped.

There was a silence, then "*Meu deus!* Jacob, my darling, where are you? You're in Rio de Janeiro? Where are you?"

"I'm here in *Ipanéma* at some hotel at the corner of *Farme de Amoeda* and *Prudente de Moraes.* I've come to find you."

They met at the entrance to the hotel, João arriving in a simple looking car with tinted windows.

"Hi, get in quickly, so many people here, not good."

They merged through the crowds, the hotel staff clearing a way through for them. Once they were out of *Ipanéma* João looked visibly more relaxed.

"It's dangerous there you know, especially for me. I mean if someone were to recognize me and my car I could be in trouble!"

"That's what I figured." Jacob answered.

"So my love has come to find me and bring me home..." João smiled.

"Yes, I've been so worried. It's been weeks, and apart from a few phone conversations we've hardly talked!"

João reached over to grab his hand, squeezing it tightly.

"Babe, I know, I'm so sorry. I just got so caught up with things here you know. Election time is coming, things are beginning to heat up and the opposition dragged me into helping them. The races are going to be tight this coming October, and they need people like me around to lay the groundwork."

"What about Eduardo? Is he running?"

"Yes he is, he may win, actually no, he will win. There is almost no way we can stop him. His mother's money is just too much."

"Too much, even for your own family?"

João laughed, "My dear, in Brazil there is always someone richer than you, who has more connections than you, and who has more ambition."

"Just like anywhere else…" retorted Jacob.

"Quite right professor Stephens."

After entering a gated community, they drove up a series of twisting, turning bends before reaching a magnificent crop of homes overlooking *Ipanéma* Beach below. João then pulled up in front of a large gate and buzzed the radiophone to be let into a small cobbled drive and parking area.

The home was magnificent, stretched out above Rio de Janeiro like out of some sort of Hollywood film from the 1960's. The palace was on two floors, its magnificent stone walls adorned with layers of ivy, and rows of French shutters opened wide, to take in the brilliant tropical sunshine.

"Wow!" was all Jacob could say.

"Mama, papa…Jacob is here!"

The next few days Professor Stephens got to know his lover's family, as they showed him about Rio de Janeiro, while opening their home to someone who had obviously done their son much good. As João's mother said, Jacob had done something to him, the gloom following David's death had given way to sparkle and happiness, and even though communication had been limited over the past two months, João never ceased to talk about his American partner.

João took Jacob out to see Rio de Janeiro, exposing him to a world he could never imagine. They wandered the cobbled twisting streets of *Santa Teresa*, they hiked the hills of the

Tijuca reserve, a gigantic Atlantic Tropical Rainforest right in the heart of the city. They visited the city centre, and its magnificent monuments, churches, theatres, coffee houses, and samba bars - all of which were a testimony to the opulence of Portuguese rule and a period of tremendous economic prosperity that was now in the past. The streets of the city were alive with the sounds of *Samba*, *Forro*, and *Bossa Nova*, as Rio de Janeiro danced and heaved its way into yet another *Carnaval.*

Jacob realized Rio de Janeiro was clearly a city full of contradictions, from rich to poor, black to white, sadness to joy, peace to violence. As João told him, while sitting together amongst the rich, the famous and the beautiful at *"Posto Nove"* on *Ipanéma Beach*, "Nothing is as it seems. In Brazil everything is an illusion, and the people on this beach; the image they present is the very essence of Brazil's illusion. The rich try to look poor so that no one will steal from them, and the poor try to look rich so that they can find acceptance."

"Ridiculous it is, yet there is no other way…this is Rio de Janeiro, and Rio is all of Brazil under one sun."

João and Jacob stayed together in Rio for six weeks, the days passing from Carnaval through Lent and into the autumn, as the scorching summer gave way to cooler, more bearable temperatures. It was also around this time that the country began to lurch towards its electoral process, as Brazil's millions prepared for state elections in the spring, with each of the candidates coming forward to present themselves for government.

There was no surprise in the news as Eduardo De Silva officially announced his intention to run for a seat in the state government, appearing at a public rally in *Botafogo*. He spoke clearly and concisely to the cameras, his good looks and athletic charm, that was so typical of the De Silva's captivating his audience.

From the comfort of the sofa, João and Jacob sat side by side in João's bedroom, staring at the younger De Silva as he charismatically reeled off his address in front of the television cameras and hoards of applauding supporters.

"So that's him."

"Yes," said João, "he's a bastard, but I can see why every woman in the world would want him."

They sat together in silence

"Your country never ceases to astound me. How can so many people be taken up with an arrogant young man from a rich family? How could they possibly believe he can solve their problems?" asked Jacob.

"When you're poor you'll believe anything, and when you're rich you'll do anything to stay rich." Answered João.

Three days later the two lovers were on the plane. Seven weeks had passed and their relationship was strongly cemented as they discovered in that time how much they needed each other. João, with Jacob's help had also made one more decision: he would take the evidence he had in New York to bring down Eduardo De Silva, not for his hatred of the man, but rather because it was time for him to softly close the door on the past, and say goodbye to his David.

Truth

Luis De Silva sat in silence at Baker's Street Café in the SOHO. It was eight fifteen in the evening and he was alone, waiting for João Nito to arrive. His mind was in overdrive as he fidgeted nervously with the napkin on the table. Just what would João be like after all that had passed? Would he have shed the last remnants of youth that he had shown whilst still with David, or would that have somehow survived the torment and pain of his partner's death?

Luis could only sit and wonder as he waited. He knew he had agreed to this meeting out of curiosity, yet there was equally an element of compassion, a profound desire to apologize to the boy who he had so coldly shaken off that fateful day two and a half years ago.

Joao appeared at the entrance to the restaurant. Tall, slender, the familiar mob of chestnut hair, and those deep thoughtful eyes, that had so understandably captured his late son. The young man was dressed in a fancy suit and tie; appropriate for the location he had chosen for their meeting. He was carrying a black leather briefcase and had a aura of confidence as he strode across the restaurant to their table.

Luis rose form his seat and reached out to give the young man a hug, "João, *faz muito tempo, que bom de ver você novamente* – it's been so long, good to see you again."

"Good to see you too sir. It has been too long, too much silence, and we need to talk, break free of the past, right?"

They stared at each for a moment, as if to study the passage of time and changes that may somehow have been visible on their faces, then took their seats.

Dinner was ordered. Both of them seemed to know the menu, laughing as they recalled their similar tastes for food, something that David had always disapproved of as a vegetarian. Wine was also chosen, as Luis left the honours for João to decide.

Finally, after some catching up and reminiscing, João turned to Luis and said, "I asked you to meet with me tonight because I believed it to be of utmost importance that you know everything that I know."

He paused, letting Luis give him his full attention before continuing. "David's murder was every bit as traumatic for me as I know it was for you, and I am sure that is why we have not been able to talk to each other since he died."

After another brief pause, he continued. "But time has passed, and enough water has flown underneath the bridge. I feel it is time I told you everything I know about David's death. There is more involved than Isabella's affair with Chico."

João continued, "David was a good man, of that we can both agree, and for that very reason there can be no possible motive for anyone to hate him, least of all some drug dealer who had no contact with him at all."

"Based on this I decided to investigate his murder. I discovered that he and Isabella Varas had indeed been the targets of some sort of a sick plot to have them eliminated. The source of that plot, which police investigations pinned to a certain dealer named Faustino, seemed entirely plausible; however, I suspected the police conclusions, since once again why would a drug dealer from the *favela* ever be interested in murdering David…"

Luis stared, silently absorbing the story João painted for him. Each time João made a new point, another piece of evidence was laid on the table between the dinner plates. Luis also understood why João had chosen this restaurant; it was quiet, their seats were private, and it was more popular with the New York Jewish crowd than any of the city's wealthier Brazilian expatriates.

"I spent immense energy and resources attempting to find out who would have possibly wanted David dead, and Isabella, Chico, Faustino, and your driver eliminated in one air-tight plot. I discovered it when a witness came forward to me after many months, producing these documents."

João pulled out several worn sheets of paper. They were wrinkled, apparently saved from some sort of a waste paper basket. Luis looked at João, about to ask if he could read the contents. João simply nodded his approval.

The minutes passed as Luis read through each of the sheets slowly, showing no emotion. The words he read were like needles in his heart, as the unimaginable was confirmed in black and white. He was deeply wounded, angered at his wife and his only remaining son, Eduardo. How could they have planned something so horrid? How could they have taken advantage of the poor and innocent Varas family to initiate such a vengeful act for pure selfish gain?

His family had struck at him through his son, stealing a life and ruining the existence of another small, yet innocent family in the sea of Brazil's aching middle class, and they had committed all this evil simply to cause more pain and anguish for Luis, so as to get more money and power for their own ambitions.

João spoke again. "I have had this on my chest for months, at least since Christmas. I decided to contact you after I learnt Eduardo was running for legislature this October, realizing you had as much a right to know as I."

Luis looked at João. They were silent; no words passing after João finished what he had to say. Then Luis spoke, "It is time we put the past behind us. I want to see more of you João, I should never have pushed you away, but those moments were so hard, and I needed to get away, away from everything."

Tears had begun to form in Luis' eyes, and he made no effort to stop them as they flowed down his cheeks.

He continued, "I lost one son that fateful day two and half years ago, and I nearly lost another, but he came back to me. I will do everything in my power to keep him close to me. João I don't want to lose you again. These papers, everything you have done, must not go to waste. I will go after those who did this, regardless of who they are, even if they are my own flesh and blood."

Overcome with emotion they sat in silence staring at the plates of unfinished food and sheets of evidence scattered across the table.

Luis then said weakly, "Damn it, let's get the hell out of this place and get some fresh air…it's too bloody stuffy here."

He then added, with more spunk, "How about ice cream? It's a summer evening and I know a great Italian *gelataria* just around the corner, Manhattan's best!"

João smiled and nodded, "Sure, the fresh air will be just perfect."

Chapter VII

Helena - Rio de Janeiro

"Good evening sir, a glass of wine?"

"Yes thank you…" answered Eduardo idly. His mind was focused on the crowds of people mingling about the gigantic gala room at the Sheraton Hotel in *Leblon.* There were easily a thousand people in the room - some of the city's most powerful and influential individuals. People like his father, people of influence and stature. Too bad the old boy had decided to cancel his attendance this year to stay on in New York.

"Silly old man," thought Eduardo. "So many business deals that could be signed amongst this elite crowd that only an idiot would ever consider passing on such a gathering."

Eduardo looked around, seeking out his mother who was here with her familiar small clique of card players, which included Eduardo's most influential supporter, the city's mayor.

"Darling, there you are! You look positively magnificent, such a handsome young man, you make your mother proud!"

"Helena, this is my son Eduardo, he's running for deputy in the state legislature elections this spring."

"Eduardo do say hello to Senhora Texeira, she's a friend of a friend." His mother paused, and continued, "I'll see you two a bit later. I have to catch up with my clan, and Eduardo, I imagine that you are sitting with some of the new nominees?"

"Yes mama I am. I'll see you after the party."

Eduardo turned back to Helena Texeira and smiled, "Pleased to meet you *madame*."

"Pleased to meet you Eduardo. Congratulations on the party nomination. I imagine you must be quite excited. Such a young man making such moves in the political world."

Eduardo smiled, blushing slightly as he looked at the rather seductive older woman in front of him. She was quite sexy, her breasts rather prominently displayed in a silk evening gown that graced her narrow hips and slender legs as they slipped out below the knee."

Eduardo could see Helena watching him look her down, and she smiled softly, causing the young man to blush even more.

"Yes, thank you Helena." He stuttered, "I am quite thrilled with the announcement, though a bit on the nervous side since I will be presented here tonight at the gala."

"Do you need someone to hold your hand?" she asked.

Eduardo coughed, laughing nervously. He looked straight at her seductive face, her piercing gaze catching his eye.

"Ah," he stammered, "I would never turn down such an offer…I imagine you are alone here tonight?"

"I am, but not anymore," she replied.

They took their seats at the new nominees table, Eduardo pulling a chair out for his impromptu date. He looked across the table, scanning the faces before him. Most of the people were unknown to him, older in every case, since he was the youngest candidate in the party. He was just about to introduce Helena and himself to everyone at the table, but before he was able to catch anyone's attention, the bells started ringing, calling everyone to take their seats.

The evening was relatively uneventful. Eduardo was not called up to talk, which pleased him, since his first speech would be kept for the following day at a smaller and more intimate "meet-the-candidate" workshop in *Botafogo*, at a local public school gym.

With dinner coming to an end, he and Helena decided to make a rush for the exits, wanting to avoid getting caught up in excessive conversation and crowds. Eduardo had left his Porsche with the executive parking on the upper deck, thus affording him quick access and a speedy exit.

Pulling out of the hotel they wound along the narrow road that took them below *Vidigal* and down into *Leblon*. Once on the open stretch of beach front boulevard, Eduardo opened up the accelerator roaring along the near empty road and crossing over the canal into *Ipanéma*. In a few short minutes they arrived at the apartment, a magnificent marble palace right in front of *Arpoador* at *Posto Oito*. The valet opened the door, taking Eduardo's Mercedes to be parked, while Eduardo and Helena walked hurriedly to the lift, riding it up to the penthouse.

"Wow, *marvilhosa esta*!" was all Helena could say as she followed Eduardo into the place.

"How can you afford such a place? Wait forgive me, you are the son of Luis De Silva." She smiled, "This is your home?"

"So many questions. No, this is not mine. It's my father's when he's in town, but it's vacant most of the time since he lives almost entirely in New York now."

"Yes I know," she sympathized. "He's been there since your brother died…tragic no?"

They walked into the living room, Eduardo taking Helena's coat and offering her a drink.

"How do you feel about that, your brother that is?"

Eduardo did not answer, preferring to ignore her question while he set about preparing two Amaretto's on ice from his father's private bar. He looked out to the living room and saw that Helena had wondered out onto the patio. She had left her shoes on the carpet and was barefoot.

"The place is magnificent…so quiet having no cars driving by in front of you. This must be the only stretch of beachfront in Rio de Janeiro that has no road in front of it," said Helena as she returned to join him in the living room.

Clasping their drinks, they sat down together in one the expensive Danish design sofas that decorated the place.

"So, a toast to your successful nomination as a new candidate!" she cried.

"Certainly!" he enthused, as Helena leaned in to kiss him on the lips.

Their embrace lasted what seemed an eternity, Helena leaning in closer to Eduardo, as their hands drifted everywhere, showing no limits. In a matter of minutes buttons, clips, and zippers were undone, as their clothes were tossed to the floor, leaving them passionately naked on the sofa, engaged in yet another of Eduardo's erotic endeavours.

Helena was a beautiful woman, and her age made her a magnificent lover, as she swept the younger less experienced man under her wing, using her long flexible legs to direct him in their passionate lovemaking. Eduardo had been with many women, but Helena seemed to know exactly what to do, using her hands to bury his face in her plump breasts while he entered her from below. The two of them were soon covered in a sheen of sweat as they rushed with animal intensity towards a wild orgasm.

Yet as soon as it had begun, it was over, and Helena was dressed and out the door and off into a taxi, leaving Eduardo alone in his father's flat, pacing about naked with a toothbrush in his mouth.

It had been an incredible night, like nothing he had ever known. Being crowned with the official party nomination and then coming to his father's palace to have sex with a magnificent woman - how privileged it was to be Eduardo De Silva.

He didn't let his thoughts wander too far though, since he knew he needed to be asleep as soon as possible so as to be in top form for his address the following day at the public school in *Botafogo*. Eduardo was also scheduled to meet his campaign manager – his mother - a bit before the address to go over any potential hiccups. Yes, he and Margaret De Silva had decided together she would work with him through the entire election; acting as his coordinator to make sure his campaign ran as flawlessly and smoothly as possible.

With his teeth clean, and his loins satisfied, he strode naked about the apartment, deciding in which room to sleep. He chose against his father's since he still respected the man, not as a father, but more for his tremendous business influence. He was about to take his old room, which was up on the second floor, when suddenly he decided the most appropriate choice would be his brother's room. "After all did he not owe his brother for all the success of the past months?" he thought.

David's adolescent room was much the same as it had always been. Maria, his father's loyal maid of many years, kept it perfect, as if she somehow believed David would magically return. The carpets were the same, including a Persian rug David had brought back from a trip to Turkey several years ago. A guitar hung from the wall, a relic from David's annoying boyfriend João Nito - the son of an upper-class family from *Leblon*. Amongst the collection of diplomas hanging from the wall, was David's Ph. D, awarded to him after his death. It was a prominent reminder of the superior intellectual abilities of his late brother.

Eduardo was suddenly overcome with fury. Anger for the fact he had never succeeded to the level of his brother, that even in death David was not only more brilliant than Eduardo, he was also more loved by their father.

He pulled David's Ph. D. from the wall, holding it in his hands, tears of rage falling from his eyes onto the glass frame. He stared at the words, written in Latin and signed by the dean. Infuriated, Eduardo threw the framed plaque against the wall, the glass cover shattering into a thousand tiny shards that glittered under the light.

He turned on his heels, grabbing the sheets from his brother's bed and walked out to the lounge, where he fell asleep on the sofa.

"Ladies and gentlemen I would like to introduce one of Brazil's youngest and most dynamic political prospects. This young man, the youngest to run in these elections, is already an established businessman in his own right, and through his father's own energies, has developed a fundamental understanding as to the needs of the State of Rio de Janeiro. This young man knows Rio de Janeiro. He knows what *Cariocas* need: jobs, security, education, and protection from crime. With great pride, I would like to introduce Eduardo De Silva."

Eduardo walked through the crowd of cheering supporters, most of them poorer voters from the suburbs, and the majority of them supporters who had been bussed in from outlying suburban communities, far from Eduardo's actual electoral district. Yet of course that didn't matter, since what was important was to have noise and crowds to create the right sorts of impressions. As he made his way to the podium he clasped the hands of men, women, and children, stopping to pose for flashing cameras.

It was perfect.

His speech was short, and held all the messages any Brazilian middle and lower class voter could possibly want to hear. He then paused, letting the applause come to a close before raising his hands to triumphantly field questions from the press.

As he looked down at the press corps, he was surprised to see Helena looking up at him, but then remembered that his mother may have said something about the woman working for *Globo News*. "I guess we'll be getting to know each other quite well over the months ahead," he thought.

"Questions anyone?"

"Yes!" shouted Helena as she rose to her feet.

Eduardo showed no hesitation in giving the woman the nod to ask the first question.

She smiled crisply, "Firstly Mr. De Silva do accept my congratulations for your impressive nomination – a phenomenal achievement for your age."

Eduardo smiled, nodding politely back.

"I would like to also convey my condolences for the loss you must feel for not being able to share this special moment with your loving brother and your father."

Eduardo nodded sympathetically, as she paused briefly. "Speaking of your late brother David De Silva, I would be interested to hear what you know about the circumstances behind his death."

Eduardo was about to brush her off and move to another reporter, but Helena interrupted him to continue, "This is important, because in my hands I have hard documents that link you, and your mother, to the murder of David De Silva, as well as to the deaths of a whole series of other innocent individuals. These same documents also show you and your mother's manipulation of police investigations, your own implications in the drug trade, and your plans to rig this election in the interest of personal gain."

Eduardo froze, the colour flowing from his face as he looked down upon the silent and expectant crowd.

"What are you talking about Miss…euhh?" he stuttered.

"Don't tell me you can't remember my name, after all we did fuck last night! Eduardo, if I may call you that, what was your involvement in the murder of your late brother David? Tell us. Tell us what these documents in my hands mean."

"Ahh…huh…" he looked over at his mother, but she was nowhere to be seen, having fled the room in panic. Overwhelmed, he bowed his head, at a loss for words.

The room erupted into pandemonium, as journalists rose to ask him more questions, hoping to cash in on a scoop of indelible proportions. Confused, he raised his hand to shield his eyes from the incessant flashing of cameras and the shouting of reporters.

Mortified and blinded, Eduardo stepped dizzily away from the podium, hurrying to escape to the nearest exit before the press could corner him.

Gasping, he rushed outside into the noisy *Botafogo* traffic, hitting a wall of soggy suffocating air. From the Rio de Janeiro sky – a billion steamy droplets of warm tropical rain exploded like diamonds, as they collided with the cracked sidewalk at his feet.

A word of thank you and some brief notes

I would like to thank the many people I have had the privilege of meeting and befriending in Latin America. Each of you in some way inspired me in the creation of this story. In particular I would like to thank Michael, Aaron, Brito, Girlaine, and Rodrigo for their kindness and compassion – I will never forget you.

A thank you to Pat and Marsha for the time and effort they so patiently put into helping me assemble this final edition. Without their guidance and patience this story would never have reached completion. I would also like to thank my mother, father, and sister, who have been there for me over the years – I love you truly.

Luis, Margaret, Eduardo, David, João, Carlos, Faustino, Jacob, Chico, Isabella, Helena, Flavio, Marcos, and the multitude of Marias – they all in some way represent each of us in their struggle for survival and self-betterment.

Favelas are the teeming slums that house approximately a third of Rio de Janeiro's inhabitants. There are some 800 favelas in "*Cidade Maravilhosa*", housing the majority of the city's lower working class – taxis drivers, policemen, maids, and service workers. This story is testimony to their's and millions of other poor people's struggle to be heard.

Botafogo, a Portuguese word meaning "to set fire", is also the name of a neighbourhood that features prominently in this novel, and was once home to one of Rio de Janeiro's most famous football teams: *Botafogo de Futebol e Regatas.* Rio de Janiero, with its stunning geographical setting, its diversity of races and religious beliefs, and its explosive mix of rich alongside poor, is indeed that: a place to set fire.

About the author

A young Jewish South African-Canadian writer and entrepreneur living on Canada's magnificent West Coast, Glen Albert Phillips was educated at *HEC Montréal* and *ESADE Barcelona* in International Business, and at the University of Victoria in Environmental Management and Chemistry. Besides English, he speaks fluent Spanish, French, and Portuguese, acquired from several years of travelling and working in some forty countries.

Glen is currently working on completing his third book, a collection of poems and short stories. Besides wandering the world, Glen also maintains an Internet journal and has produced a compilation of poems, some of which he has put to guitar.

A special thanks is in order to his sister, Nicole S. Phillips, who created the 1st edition book cover. Her work is available at www.visualheart.com.

Printed in Great Britain
by Amazon

56840512R00088